She was late, and ~~get rid of her hic~~ **Suddenly there w**
door. . . .

Maybe her neighbor Melda could help her. Only partially dressed, she threw open the door. Hawk Dyhart stood there, a smile on his lips that made her want to give up on getting dressed. "I have to go out," she said lamely.

"You don't look ready," he said, propping himself against the door.

"I'm not. I'm in such a hurry, I can't get it right."

"Let me help." He pushed away from the door and urged her back into her room. Her hands tightened on the fabric of her pareau, and she was irritated to see his eyes light with amusement.

"I don't see how you can," she said firmly. She stifled a gasp as he took hold of her pareu, turned her about, and swathed the fabric around her body so that one piece drifted over her shoulder and fastened perfectly. How had he done it so fast? She turned to the mirror, unwillingly admiring the fluid lines of the garment. "How many women do you dress every day?" she muttered, then felt embarrassed when she realized she'd spoken aloud. She wanted to sink through the floorboards.

He slipped his arms around her waist. "Not many, actually, but I'd like to volunteer to dress you." His gaze dropped to her mouth as she bit her lip. "I'd like to do that too."

"What?"

"Bite your lip." He kissed her ear. "Nibble you all over."

"Oh," she murmured. "Cannibal. . . ."

WHAT ARE *LOVESWEPT* ROMANCES?

They are stories of true romance and touching emotion. We believe those two very important ingredients are constants in our highly sensual and very believable stories in the *LOVESWEPT* line. Our goal is to give you, the reader, stories of consistently high quality that may sometimes make you laugh, sometimes make you cry, but are always fresh and creative and contain many delightful surprises within their pages.

Most romance fans read an enormous number of books. Those they truly love, they keep. Others may be traded with friends and soon forgotten. We hope that each *LOVESWEPT* romance will be a treasure—a "keeper." We will always try to publish

LOVE STORIES YOU'LL NEVER FORGET
BY AUTHORS YOU'LL ALWAYS REMEMBER

The Editors

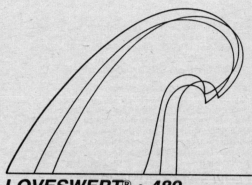

LOVESWEPT® • 489

Helen Mittermeyer

A Moment in Time

BANTAM BOOKS
NEW YORK • TORONTO • LONDON • SYDNEY • AUCKLAND

A MOMENT IN TIME
A Bantam Book / August 1991

If you would be interested in receiving protective vinyl
covers for your Loveswept books, please write to this address
for information:

Loveswept
Bantam Books
P.O. Box 985
Hicksville, NY 11802

ISBN 0-553-44153-1

Published simultaneously in the United States and Canada

PRINTED IN THE UNITED STATES OF AMERICA

OPM 0 9 8 7 6 5 4 3 2 1

One

Hawksworth Dyhart stretched and yawned, turning his face up to the sun. Reveling in the solace of the tropical heat, he felt his work-tense body relax as his gaze flickered out over the sea.

Instantly, his glance sharpened. He saw the swimmer and the telltale fin at the same time. He shut his eyes against the glare of sun and water, then opened them again, fixing on the same point. It hadn't been a mirage. The swimmer was out too far, beyond the wreck that usually drew the tourists on this coast of Barbados.

"Hey!" he called. "Can't you see?"

His loud shout cut through the boom of the surf and the screeching of the gulls. Alarmed birds rose in noisy swarms overhead, dipping and swaying in angry rebuttal, but the swimmer stroked on parallel to the shore, oblivious to the danger.

Cursing, Hawk stripped off his pajama bottoms, his only clothing, and sprinted for a water scooter pulled up on shore. This damn well hadn't been part of his plan for some rest and relaxation in Barbados. Gritting his teeth, he turned the handle on the scooter, once, twice. The engine coughed, then roared. He raised the handles for maximum speed, and the sudden thrust almost unbalanced him. He didn't have much experience with scooters, but his strength and determination soon had him speeding toward his target. Though the scooter bucked over the waves as though jet-propelled, the short distance seemed miles away. Could he beat the shark to its intended kill? He shuddered at the alternative, his naked body beading with cold sweat.

As he skimmed over the water, he opened the scooter to full throttle, risking a tumble into the sea for himself. Aiming at a point midway between the shark and the swimmer, he tried to calculate just how much clearance he'd need, how big and determined the shark was, what the size of its intended victim was. He would have to try to grab the swimmer with one hand and steer the scooter with the other. The idea was fraught with danger. He could smash into the person he intended to rescue, or tip them both into the sea off the unsteady scooter.

Slowing down fractionally for better control, he bent his body low as he neared the swimmer. Out of the corner of his eye he thought he saw the gray fin, but he couldn't be sure. He gripped the control hard with his right hand, then leaned far over to grab the swimmer with his left arm.

The jerk of his arm as he lifted the victim seemed almost to wrench his shoulder from its socket. The scooter rocked perilously, and the muscles of his right arm bulged as he fought to keep the water vehicle from tipping. The swimmer—who was a woman, he'd realized instantly—struggled against him, flailing and taking in water as he pulled her partially onto the scooter. "What're you doing?" she shouted.

Hawk was having too much trouble balancing the scooter to answer. With adrenaline-born strength, he managed the almost impossible task of turning the scooter around and speeding back toward shore. He tried not to picture the shark chasing after them. His writhing passenger was yelling and glaring at him, but he couldn't hear a word she said over the roaring motor. She probably hadn't realized her danger, he thought. As they rapidly neared the shore, he knew he was going to have a hard time stopping the scooter with one hand. He could fall off with his passenger into the water. Were they over coral yet?

"Stay still!" he yelled, but his bellow faded into the wind. As the shore loomed closer, he thought of releasing his hold on the handle, but didn't. Letting go completely could be dangerous over coral. Where was the shark?

Too fast. Hawk braced himself as they zoomed

out of the water and onto the sand. They banged and screeched to a stop. Every tooth in his head rattled, his grip on the handle released. Flung over the top of the scooter, he and the woman plowed into the sand, rolling over and over, collecting bits of coral, shells, and sand on every portion of their bodies.

Hawk ended up facedown in the sand. Lifting his head, he barely had time to spit out some coral when he saw the fist aimed at his face. Pulling back was the only thing that saved him from a solid hit to the jaw. As it was the woman's fist grazed his eye, slamming his head back.

"Dammit!" he yelled. "What the hell's the matter with you? I just saved your life."

Holding one hand to his face, he rolled up onto his knees, staring out of his other eye at the ungrateful woman he'd just saved. Clad in a skintight one-piece bathing suit and dripping seawater, she glared furiously at him. Her ebony hair hung in sandy strands around her face. Her rounded but slender figure was coated with sand, pieces of shell, some dried seaweed, and bits of driftwood. Though she wasn't tall, her legs were long and shapely. Under that coating of grit he glimpsed satiny, creamy skin. As he studied her face, he realized she was astonishingly beautiful. He especially liked her nose. There was a tiny hook to it, giving it a slight aquiline cast. Her eyes were green jewels rayed with gold, and they glittered gemlike in her anger. She was lovely . . . intriguing . . . And a damned ingrate.

"You're naked!" she exclaimed, her scowl deepening.

"I damn well wasn't going to don a shirt and tie to save your life," he shot back. His eye was beginning to throb.

"Saved my life, did you? You hammerhead, I wasn't in any danger. I've been snorkeling and diving for years and—"

"There was a shark after you," interrupted Hawk, getting to his feet, his hand still pressed to his eye. He saw how she scanned him, then pointedly looked away. He was shocked to realize his body was eager to respond to her searing gaze. He hung on to his righteous anger to prevent that. "There," he said. "Out there. See for yourself." He pointed at the fin. It hadn't moved much. "A shark!"

She spun around and studied the sea, one hand shading her face. "Where?"

Hawk saw another head break the surface near the gray fin. "That other swimmer's in danger. . . ." He ran to the water's edge. Cupping his hands around his mouth, he shouted "Shark!"

A hand came down hard on his arm, pulling it away from his face. "Will you stop yelling? You'll scare the guests." The woman looked around the beach, then back at him. "And get some clothes on before you really panic them."

Hawk scowled down at her, even as a part of him noted how sexy she looked, despite the sand that covered her. "I'm warning him about the shark." He pointed again at the gray fin.

"Stupid. That's not a shark, it's a flag. We didn't have an orange one, so Dandy put out that gray one. It's not a kosher marker, but it was all we had. A gray flag. That's your shark's fin." She tapped him on the chest with one sand-coated finger. "You dragged me out of the water, skinned me up on the shore, rolled me in the sand and coral, and for what? I could've cut myself to ribbons because you can't tell a flag from a fin." Glaring at him, she poked him again in the chest. Her voice rose. "Are you out of your ever-loving mind?"

"You're the one disturbing the guests now," Hawk muttered, fighting back his embarrassment. He looked out to sea once more and saw the other diver waving from right next to the gray flag. "It damn well looks like a fin. You shouldn't have substituted another color."

The woman again glanced at the hotel guests moving their way, drawn by the commotion. "Will you get dressed?" she whispered fiercely. "You're making a fool of yourself. Nude swimming isn't allowed here."

Hawk glared at her. She glared back. Tart-tongued brat, he thought as he turned and stalked away. He'd stuck out his neck to save her. And he'd made a fool of himself. Cursing steadily, he stomped back to his condo, ignoring the stares and his pajama bottoms crumpled on the beach.

Someone whistled. Grinding his teeth, Hawk stormed up the narrow path leading to his somewhat-secluded condo. He flung open the door, then banged it shut behind him.

Dandy swam to shore, then walked backward up onto the beach in his flippers. "Did my eyes deceive me," he asked the dark-haired woman still standing there, "or was that a nude guest you were talking to?"

"It's wasn't a guest," Bahira Massoud said through her teeth. "It was a blasted loony." Still, she acknowledged reluctantly, it had taken courage for him to rescue her from what he thought was a shark. He had great buns too.

Dandy looked her up and down. "You look awful. Been dragged through a dumpster?"

"Very funny." Bahira brushed ineffectually at the debris and sand covering her. "That fool thought our gray flag was a shark fin, and he roared out in a scooter to save me. Darn near dislocated my entire body, the way he grabbed me. Then he whirled me around and banged back up on the beach, tossing me right over the front of the scooter." She pointed to the furrow she'd made in the sand. "I could've broken my neck!"

Dandy's white teeth flashed briefly in his dark face, then he frowned. "We'd better get rid of that flag. One of the guests might get the same idea as your Lone Ranger."

Bahira nodded. "Let's go get the equipment. I'm done for the day."

"You'd better put some ointment on those

scrapes," Dandy said. "After you shower, of course."

Bahira made a face at her friend, then she ran into the sea, groaning as the saltwater stung the many small abrasions on her skin.

Later that afternoon, when Bahira went on duty at the front desk of the Grand Bajian hotel, her mind was still fixed on the handsome Adonis who didn't know a shark's fin from a flag. No doubt being that good-looking, he didn't need brains, she thought. It annoyed her that she hadn't been able to get the sexy donderhead out of her mind all day.

Lavinia, the day-shift clerk, grinned at her as Bahira slipped around to the back of the desk. "You missed it."

Bahira smiled, knowing her friend must be talking about a man. Lavinia loved men. "Tom Cruise arrive?" she asked.

"Almost as good. Hawk Dyhart is in the Coral Cottage." Lavinia said with a sigh, referring to the Grand Bajian's most expensive and secluded condominium. "He came in when Trudy was on at *five in the morning.*"

"Whoopee," Bahira said dryly, then laughed when Lavinia looked disappointed. "I don't know who Hawk Dyhart is."

"That's because you don't read the tabloids." Lavinia grinned. "You're uneducated, Bahira. Dyhart is from Chicago and owns a big industrial company, Dyhart International Tool and

Die. And he's in banking too. I read about him when he testified at one of those savings-and-loan trials in Washington, D.C. Remember?"

"Oh. He's a famous crook," Bahira said, and grinned at her friend's indignant look. Now that she thought about it though, Hawk Dyhart's name was familiar. She'd seen it in the papers once or twice, but she couldn't recall why. Most of the time she tried not to read about monetary scandals. It brought back too many painful memories.

"He's not a crook!" Lavinia exclaimed. "He was a witness in one of the cases." Her mouth rounded in awe. "But I'll bet he knows some crooks." She looked at her watch and yelped. "I'll be late. See you tomorrow, Bahira."

"All right." Though they were friends, Bahira was glad Lavinia left. Her words had brought back a painful episode in Bahira's life. Her uncle, who had raised her after her parents died when she was young, and his son had been accused of bankrupting their own investment company for unlawful gain. Eventually, they had been cleared of the charges, but it had left its mark on the family. They'd lost the company, and all the liquid assets. She, her uncle, and her cousin had been wiped out. Bahira had had to drop out of graduate school, where she'd almost completed her master's in biology, while her uncle and cousin struggled to rebuild the company. She had learned how to fend for herself, become self-supporting, but she missed her family very much. Seeing a guest approach the registration desk, Bahira shook her head to clear it of the black thoughts and smiled. "Good day, sir. May I help you?"

Wide, well-muscled shoulders, thick chestnut hair with red highlights, sexy hands, and golden eyes filled Bahira's dreams that night. Even as she told herself he was probably one of those too rich, too spoiled people who owned resort homes along the beach, not someone she had anything in common with, she couldn't banish him from her mind.

Had it been her imagination, she wondered as she struggled to wake up, that his body had been somewhat aroused when they'd been together? That was insane. He hadn't been. Had he? Bahira tried thinking of her grocery list, sorting her laundry, but still the vivid picture of Tall, Naked, and Sexy was there.

She swung out of bed, her feet hitting the cool floor. Groaning, she rose, stretched, and grimaced. She disliked the first day of a new shift. Today, she began two weeks of the morning shift, after coming off two weeks of the night shift. She felt fatigued and somewhat disoriented.

Dragging herself into the shower, she let the water sluice over her far longer than she normally did before shampooing and washing. After drying off, she dressed speedily because she was several minutes late. She left her room on the run, jumping down the two flights of stairs two at a time. Running through a large, flower-filled courtyard, she grabbed a croissant off the bread cart outside an open-air restaurant. Biting into its flaky warmth, she hurried down the winding path that led to the wall-less lobby.

"Bahira, why don't you get fat?" the clerk still on duty asked. "I do if I eat those."

Bahira grinned. "You're not fat, Althea. Dandy thinks you're perfect. I'm sorry I'm late."

Althea smiled, pointing at the clock. "You're not." She waved as she walked away from the desk. "See you."

Bahira waved back absently, then checked the guest book, the reservations list, the computer data. Suddenly, her mind did a nosedive and the picture of a wide chest with a patch of chestnut hair superimposed itself over the computer monitor. Stop that! she ordered her giddy imagination. When had she turned so silly? She had a serious mission in life, supporting herself and sending what money she saved to her uncle Mohammar to help him rebuild his company. She certainly didn't have time to dwell on a naked knight with golden eyes.

Hawk was restless. Impulse had brought him to Barbados. He'd been feeling edgy, though he didn't know why. He had no reason to be disenchanted with anything.

He stared out the large window of his living room at the sun-dappled sea. Paradise. He'd kick back for the next two weeks, do some sailing, swimming, diving. Forget about business.

He shrugged his shoulders as though to dislodge a weight. Why the dissatisfaction? he wondered. It was crazy to be in Bardados in the middle of July. He could have stayed in Chicago if he wanted heat. They were having it in spades. His business was in excellent shape. They'd handled the diversification into the communications field with a minimum of fuss. He'd begun dating a wealthy socialite who promised to be as exciting in bed as she was haughty in public. He enjoyed perfect health, and was still—though just barely—on the sunny side of forty. There were no serious problems in his life, nothing insurmountable, nothing that couldn't be handled.

Except . . . he touched his slightly puffy eye. Except that firecracker who'd torn his head off when he'd tried to rescue her. From a gray flag. He grimaced. Then he chuckled when he thought of how they'd spiraled through the air when the scooter had halted abruptly in the sand. Lord! When she'd turned to face him, she'd been spitting mad. Covered with sand and shells and debris from the crown of her head to her toes, she'd been the messiest beauty he'd ever seen. Angry and sexy as hell.

Even as her temper had fired his, he'd been aware of her beauty. He didn't think he'd ever seen black-green eyes like hers. He chuckled remembering how she'd looked him over as if he were something she'd scraped off her shoe. And if her gaze had lingered just an instant longer, he would have been thoroughly aroused. Then she'd have really torn a strip off him. Even in the short time he'd held her, he'd realized her body was wonderfully formed. Who, he wondered, was she?

He turned to stare at his open briefcase, papers spilling out of it and onto the desk. His early enthusiasm for work had waned. He had to do something to get that little termagant off his mind. He could go into Bridgetown. Or perhaps go sailing. He'd never stayed at this particular hotel before, and he abruptly decided to go out to the front desk to see what was available.

Dressed in bathing trunks, a string shirt, and leather slip-ons, Hawk left his condo, the Coral Cottage. The wide path led past the open air restaurant called The Shell, then twisted around and through a Japanese garden that formed the courtyard for the largest section of accommodations. His place was the most private, the most remote from all others and the lobby.

Surrounded by clusters of flaming red and pink frangipani and hibiscus, he inhaled deeply. The breeze that wafted in from the sea was redolent of ginger and cinnamon. Peace and quiet, he thought as he exhaled. That would settle his restlessness.

As he approached the long bamboo-sided reservation desk, he saw the clerk was preoccupied, writing something, her head bent down. Satin black hair curtained her face. He stopped in front of her, and she looked up. The same surprise that flashed across her face must have been on his. The green-eyed beauty from the day before was a desk clerk. Hawk recovered first. "Your mouth is open, Miss—" he glanced at her name tag—"Massoud. And you dropped your pen." He handed it back to her. "I'm Hawk Dyhart in the Coral Cottage."

She closed her eyes as though she had a sudden headache, then forced a smiled onto her lips. "Mr. Dyhart," she said in a strained voice. "How may I help you, sir?"

"A number of ways, I'm sure," he murmured, watching the slow run of red up her neck. Her black-green eyes glittered like precious emeralds. They were crackling with ire, despite her smile. He knew she was at a disadvantage. She couldn't talk back to a guest. Baiting her was unfair . . . but too much fun to resist. "For now," he went on, "I'd like to rent some diving equipment, and I'd like to make reservations for dinner. Is there a concierge?"

"I can handle it here, sir."

"Perhaps you can show me the best places to dive too," he said.

She stiffened at his blatant reminder of their first meeting, and he bit back his smile. Now that he was able to study her without the camouflage of the sand and shells, he could reaffirm his first impression. She was a stunner. Her wonderful skin was like cream silk, and when she blushed, it turned a beckoning rose hue.

"We have an expert on the diving places in our

area," she said woodenly. "Dandy Jordan would be glad to help you."

"Fine." Hawk grinned at her. She was flaming mad again. She was also as beautiful, colorful, and exotic as Barbados itself. She talked like an American, looked like an American, but there were subtle differences that made him wonder if she might be from the Middle East or North Africa. She was taller and slimmer than many of the women from those areas. Her hips were rounded but not wide, her breasts uptilted. Her skin was pinky cream, not olive, and stretched over high cheekbones and an almost pointed chin. And she shouldn't have those unusual eyes. He wanted to talk to her, coax her out from behind the desk. She had a quick temper, a tongue like a scythe . . . and a womanliness that rolled off her in waves, as though all the secrets of Eve and Venus were hers. He looked at her name tag again. "Bahira is a beautiful name. Is it Iranian?"

"No, Moroccan, sir. Would you like me to call Dandy and ask if he's free?"

He inclined his head, acknowledging her change of subject. "Do that . . . please."

His husky voice seemed to smooth over Bahira's skin, raising goose bumps. Don't look at him, she told herself. After the way she'd lit into him the previous afternoon, he could get her fired. When she lifted the phone, she had to stiffen all of her muscles to keep her hand from shaking.

"I could send him to your condo, sir," she said,

and risked a glance at him. His cream-colored string shirt showed off a tan that looked as if it had been his since birth. His strong arms hung from powerful shoulders. He looked more like a football player than a businessman. And if he didn't leave soon, she would crack every tooth in her mouth. She stared for a moment at his left eye. It was slightly swollen and bluish. Oh, Lord.

"That's all right," he said. "I'll wait here." He leaned on the desk, closer to her, beaming at her.

"As you wish." Biting her lip, she dialed Dandy's extension. When he answered, she briefly explained Hawk Dyhart's request. Dandy said he would be right there.

Minutes ticked by, the silence stretching like a frayed rubber band threatening to snap. The old fashioned wag-on-the-wall clock behind Bahira thumped loudly. The wind crackling through the royal palms was deafening.

Hawk watched her and remembered how she'd looked like a beautiful, vengeful sea goddess.

Bahira tried not to recall his wonderful bare body and limbs.

"Hi, Bahira," Dandy called as he crossed the lobby.

Relief scudded through her. The rigidity melted out of Bahira's spine, and she almost slipped to the floor. "Dandy! At last," she breathed.

Dandy's smile faltered as Hawk laughed heartily. "You only called me a few minutes ago."

"Seemed like hours," Bahira muttered, ignoring the still-chuckling Hawk Dyhart. "Our guest, Mr. Dyhart, would like to be shown some choice diving areas. Now."

Dandy turned to the guest, smiling. Bahira realized with relief that Dandy didn't recognize him as the nude man from the beach. "Ready, sir?" Dandy asked.

"Yes," Hawk murmured, still looking at Bahira.

"I think Miss Massoud wants us to go."

Bahira counted to ten, then twenty. Dyhart could have her fired. She needed her job. She could be charming. And he'd soon be gone. "Enjoy your dive, sir."

"I will." Hawk stared at her for a moment longer. She was an exquisite madonna with the temperament of Napoleon. It was on the tip of his tongue to ask when she had free time, but he was sure she'd freeze him out. "See you soon, Miss Massoud," he said instead. Her smile almost fell off her face, but she managed to hang on to it.

"You will like our waters, sir," Dandy said as they walked from the lobby. "The sharks and moray eel are very friendly to the tourists."

Hawk glanced at his grinning companion. "And do they bother you, Dandy?"

"No, sir. We have an understanding. When I dive, I ask their permission first." Dandy waved his arm, directing his guest along the path to the beach. "If you're checked out on scuba, I'll get you gear for that as well as snorkeling, sir."

"I'm checked out on scuba. Thank you, Dandy." They stopped at a small shed, and Hawk gazed out at the water, admiring the panoply of sailboats and other craft. "You handle all the boats, too, Dandy?"

The other man nodded. "Me and some of the others. Most of us have more than one job in the hotel, sir."

"Even the desk clerk, Miss Massoud?"

Dandy studied him for a moment, then nodded slowly. "Oh, yes. Sometimes Bahira helps with the tours, arranging them and even going along as a guide or companion." Dandy grinned. "We can make extra money on our off time that way."

"Good idea. How would I go about setting up a tour? I'd be more interested in something private, rather than being part of a group."

"You can talk to the desk," Dandy said as he pulled scuba gear from the shed, "or you can get in touch with the tour people yourself. There's a list of them in your room, in the book next to the phone."

"Great. Maybe I'll call them," Hawk said. He saw the sudden sharp look Dandy gave him.

"Bahira Massoud is my friend," Dandy said softly, "and a friend to my wife. We think of her as family."

Hawk eyed the man and nodded. "I'd like to get some diving done." Noting the tightening of Dandy's mouth, he knew he was being too abrupt. But he had no answer for the man. Nor did he know why he'd questioned him about a tour. He did know he wanted to see Bahira Massoud again. The urgency of that feeling unsettled him. How could he explain to Dandy Jordon something he didn't quite understand himself?

The diving was better than good. It was great. Out beyond the first wreck was an undersea world that fascinated Hawk. He did see a moray eel and a barracuda, but neither approached, and he gave them a wide berth.

Back on shore Hawk shook Dandy's hand. "Do you think we might go out tomorrow?" he asked.

Dandy smiled and nodded, then began stowing the gear in the shed.

Hawk jogged down the beach, feeling energized and relaxed. The dive had been just what he needed. When he reached his condo, he stripped off his trunks, intending to take a long shower. He hesitated, though, staring at the small directory beside the phone. Leafing through it, he found the list of names he looked for, chose one, then dialed.

Bahira had a jumbled day. She managed to check in the guests without too many mistakes, but a face kept jumping onto the computer screen, distracting her. She'd watched Hawk Dyhart until he'd left the lobby with Dandy, and that image had stayed with her. The guest register listed him as Hawksworth Dyhart, but he'd introduced himself as Hawk. And he was one. His gaze could melt coral.

As the day wore on, she found herself wondering what he was doing. Scouting Bridgetown for beautiful women? Lunching with a beautiful woman? Thinking about the hotel clerk who'd berated him . . . ?

"Hi, Bahira."

The voice of the woman who had the afternoon shift startled Bahira, and she stared at her dark-skinned colleague.

"Sorry I'm a little late," Loula said nervously. "Are you mad at me?"

Bahira blinked, trying to focus on the other woman.

"Oh. No, I'm not angry. I was just thinking about something. Don't worry, Loula. I wasn't in any hurry." In fact, she hadn't even realized Loula was twenty minutes late.

"Thanks, Bahira. You're a peach." Loula looked relieved. Like Bahira, she needed her job.

Bahira smiled weakly. "Don't worry about it." She'd spent a good deal of her shift thinking about a man who could get her fired if he decided to complain. She had much more reason to worry than the habitually late Loula.

"You sure you're okay?" Loula asked. "You look a little pale."

Bahira avoided her friend's gaze as she walked around to the front of the desk. "I'm fine. Honest."

"Okay," Loula said doubtfully. "See you later."

Bahira walked blindly across the lobby, feeling

as though she'd been parasailing and the engine on the pull boat had stalled. She was hurtling to the sea under collapsed wings of silk, drowning and smothering in silliness. The man stuck in her mind because he annoyed her, she told herself, and for no other reason. She was acting like a teenager with a crush. Disgusted, she strode quickly across the courtyard toward her quarters.

Maybe she was just lonely, she mused. She should call her cousin Karim and her uncle Mohammar. Just talking to them would be the magic touch that lifted her spirits.

She raced up the stairs to her tiny apartment, and had just put the key in the door when she heard her phone begin to ring. She hurried inside and picked up the receiver. "Yes?" she said, a little breathlessly.

"Bahira? It's Loula. I just got a call from the tour-bus people. Someone asked for you specifically for tomorrow night. How about that? Shall I set it up?"

"Sure. I can use the money. Thanks, Loula." She cradled the phone and looked out her window at the back of the complex. Her balcony didn't overlook the sea, it overlooked the dumpster.

In her bathroom she stripped off her clothes and dropped them in the hamper. She'd have to go to the Laundromat soon, she thought. As she stepped into the shower, she deliberately shut everything from her mind—especially the guest in the Coral Cottage. But it wasn't easy.

• • •

After her shower Bahira looked longingly at her bed. She needed sleep to banish the shocks of yesterday and today—being manhandled by a naked man and then finding out he was a guest. Lord!

Yes, sleep was what she needed, but first she'd try to contact her uncle and cousin. The time difference would put them at around the lunch hour in Los Angeles. She dialed the number of Massoud, Inc., and the receptionist picked up on the first ring. She put Bahira straight through to her cousin, since her uncle was out at a business lunch.

Karim was pleased to hear from her. They exchanged news, and he told her that both he and his father were in good health, and that the business was doing well. They didn't talk long, however, since the call was so expensive. Bahira ended the conversation by telling Karim to give Uncle Mohammar her love. When she replaced the receiver, she had to wipe away a few tears, as always. She was so far away from Los Angeles. The Massouds no longer traveled hither, thither, and yon on a whim. They were struggling, like millions of other working-class people. They were no longer a wealthy branch of the Moroccan aristocracy.

Though she was now on the bottom struggling to raise herself, Bahira wasn't unhappy with her life. Nor had the transition been as horrible as she'd feared. She felt good, capable, competitive. She liked supporting herself, and hotel work was fun. Maybe it wasn't the biological research she'd pictured for her future, but life was enjoyable, and she felt very much a part of the American mainstream. If only she weren't so far from her family.

Sighing, she slipped between her cotton sheets. She'd eat dinner after her nap. And in the morning she'd be better adjusted to her new schedule, and would rise at five for her swim.

She fell asleep as her head hit the pillow.

Two

A gull crying in the predawn woke Bahira. She groaned, shook her head, and opened one eye. Ghostly gray light crept in her window. Oh, Lord! she thought. She'd missed dinner and slept right through the night. She yawned hugely, then she rubbed her middle. She was hungry, but first things first. She'd better work out, or she'd be logy all day.

It was the perfect time for a swim. Few guests would be about, the water would be crisp, the air sweet and warm, but not hot. These next two days would be busy. Tonight she'd take out the tour. Tomorrow she'd go to Dandy and Althea's for their dinner party. They'd been her first real friends on the island.

She scrambled into her one-piece bathing suit, then pulled on a pair of nylon shorts and a faded T-shirt. Hitching her beach bag and towel over her shoulder, she left her one-room apartment with its postage stamp–sized bathroom, quietly closing the door behind her and locking it.

After skipping down the two flights of stairs, she sprinted across the inner courtyard of the guest apartments to the beach, jogging on to a small cove. She always spent time in the private area where few guests ventured.

Spotting Dandy at the far end of the beach, she waved and smiled. The gray light was fading fast, and Bahira predicted the day would be bright and pristine. The Caribbean would roll in sheer blue swells. The wind was settling to a soft breeze that made the palm fronds crackle like rain on a tin roof, the sound not abrasive but comforting.

She dived into the sea and swam hard and fast for fifteen minutes. As she was drying herself, Dandy approached, carrying a pair of swim fins and a mask. His T-shirt with the torn-off sleeves proclaimed him A RENAISSANCE MAN. "Hi," he said. "Day shift?"

"Yep. Then a tour tonight. I'll see you and Althea tomorrow night."

He nodded. "Right. Gotta go for the money." He squinted at her, the morning sun slanting off his face. "Something on your mind?"

Dandy's ability to read her moods was disconcerting sometimes, but at the moment Bahira welcomed someone to talk to. She bent to scoop up some sand, letting it run through her fingers. "Remember the man who pulled the Superman-to-the-rescue caper with the water scooter?"

"Sure, I remember." Dandy smiled. "You tore a strip off him."

Bahira grinned ruefully. "I did. And I was wrong when I said he wasn't a guest. He's staying in the Coral Cottage."

Dandy shoved back his hat. "Whoa."

"I don't know why I didn't figure he was a guest. I just didn't think. Then I blew my top, to put the icing on the cake." She smiled worriedly at her friend. "He could have me fired, Dandy."

"Maybe he'll forget about it," Dandy said hopefully. "He might just laugh it off."

"And he might not." She took a deep breath. "He was the guest you took out yesterday afternoon, Hawk Dyhart."

"Oh, Lord."

She shook her head. "I can't believe I belted him." She glanced at her watch. "I have to go."

Dandy patted her arm. "Don't worry."

"Right." Bahira jogged back toward the staff apartments, and the image of Hawk Dyhart accompanied her. She could clearly see his strong, muscular body with sleek, long legs, his smile with one tiny dimple, his chestnut hair with auburn streaks. The man was lethal in more ways than one. Yes, he could have her fired, but he could do worse. He could lodge himself in her heart and never leave.

Hawk watched Bahira race up the beach. He had decided to take an early morning swim, and he hadn't counted on seeing the woman who'd danced in his mind all the previous day and through his dreams that night. The natural, unconsciously sexy sway of her hips caught his attention and held it. She was beautifully made, with such creamy skin, intriguing eyes . . . and a tongue that could slice wood. He wanted to know more about her, and he would, that night.

Hawk grinned as he strode to the water. He was looking forward to the evening, to his tour with Bahira. And wouldn't she raise hell about that.

Late that afternoon Bahira took extra care preparing for her evening tour. After showering, she painted her fingernails and toenails a pale coral color. It was the same hue as one of the flowers in the patterned pareau she'd be wearing. The background was sea green and the swaths of coral and cream gave it a Barbadian dash.

Was Hawk Dyhart showering? she wondered as she began to dress. Had he shampooed that rich, thick chestnut-hued hair? She tried not envision him naked, rubbing his head with a towel, but she could see him as clearly as though he stood in front of her. And he had stood in front of her . . . naked. Blindly, she stared into her mirror, imagining him moving toward her. Her body arced in unconscious desire as though to be closer to him, and goose bumps rose on her skin. She felt hot, aroused. . . . The reprobate! she thought. How could he enter her head like that? Crossing her arms over her naked breasts, she took deep breaths to calm herself. "Stop it, Bahira," she whispered, and the sound of her voice shattered the moment.

Glancing at the clock, she yelped. Time had got away from her. *Hic!* Oh, no, she thought. Not hiccups. Not now. That always happened to her when she was upset. Hawk Dyhart was going to give her an ulcer.

Flipping the cotton pareau around her body, she cinched it under her breasts, making it strapless and leaving her shoulders, neck, and arms bare. The soft material dropped straight down her body, ending a couple of inches above her feet. Those were shod in turquoise and coral-colored sandals that she'd found in a flea market in Bridgetown.

Hic!

She held her breath until she turned red.

Hic!

She slashed coral lipstick across her mouth and grabbed her cotton-knit bag. Snatching up her key, she slammed out of the apartment.

Hic!

Hopping down the stairs two at a time, she passed one of the cleaning ladies. "Hi, Nanta. Have a nice evening." *Hic!*

"Slow up, Bahira," the black woman said, smiling and shaking her head. "All that rushing's giving you the belly rumbles. You be careful on them stairs, you'll break your neck."

"I'll get there, Nanta. 'Bye." Bahira waved but

didn't slow down. Sprinting across the courtyard, she lost one of her sandals, and was several feet past it before she could stop. Retrieving it took many more precious moments. Oh, Lord, she thought, what time was she to meet the guests? *Hic!* She should be early.

She skated around some beautiful frangipani into the open-sided lobby. A few guests and LeRoy, the night clerk, gaped at her. She shrugged, smiled weakly, then walked hurriedly through the lobby to the path that led to the front area of the hotel. Tour guests always met there. *Hic!*

"You've got the hiccups," a voice said in her ear. "Slow down."

Dyhart! Bahira thought. What was he doing there? "Good evening, sir," she said over her shoulder. "Excuse me. I have some guests to meet."

She crossed to the desk on the far side of the waiting area and grabbed the reservation book. Scanning the page, she saw her name at the top of a column. But underneath it, instead of the names of several guests, she saw only one name. Hawk Dyhart. Looking up, she stared right into his leonine eyes.

"You're blushing, Miss Massoud," he said. "Something wrong?"

"Ah, no. I'm fine." *Hic!*

"Except for hiccups."

"Ah, I'd be happy to discuss—*hic*—the problem, but I'm . . ." What? she wondered. What possible excuse could she give to get out of this?

"I'm the person you'll be taking on the tour," he said. "I asked for you specifically." She hic-cupped again and pressed a hand to her middle. "Tummy upset?" he asked.

"It will be," she said darkly, then grimaced. Why did she always say the wrong thing to him? With the other guests she was more than smooth. Hawk Dyhart was two kinds of a devil, the spawn of Satan's knee, as Uncle Mohammar would say. It certainly wasn't her fault that he brought out the worst in her, made her temper flare, made her say things she shouldn't. "I think we could call the desk," she began without much hope, "and ask if any of the other guests might like to join—"

"No," he said easily. "This is fine. I've paid for all the seats."

"Extravagant." *Hic!*

"A good slap square on the back sometimes works," he said helpfully. "Would you like me to try?"

"No . . . thank you." She gazed at him cau-tiously. He had eyes like lasers. If she looked down, would there be an *H* burned on her pareau? *Hic!*

"I think the bus is this way." Taking hold of her upper arm, he steered her out of the roofed area and down the curving path to the taxi stand.

His hold was gentle, but it did crazy things to Bahira's insides. Her stomach flip-flopped. She saw red lights and stars in front of her eyes. Her skin tingled as if she had frostbite. Her reaction to him embarrassed and upset her, and she lashed out at him. "I don't need to be trolled like a hooked shark behind a boat." *Hic!* Lord, she was too sharp. He was a guest!

"Breathe deeply," Hawk advised, laughter coiling through him. Her annoyance at herself and him amused him. She had to struggle to keep her professional smile in place, and it would give him extreme pleasure to knock it askew. Bahira Massoud was lemon and cinnamon. He hadn't even known that spicy flavor was necessary to his life before he met her. He looked forward to the evening, and he allowed himself a chuckle of pleasure.

"You laugh at the strangest times," she said, staring up at him.

He gazed back at her, watching a flush darken her creamy skin. What was she thinking? he wondered. He watched the intriguing way her features seemed to stiffen, as if she were pulling in on herself. "You're blushing," he said softly.

"Genetic weakness," she mumbled. "Mother had it."

"I see." He slipped his hand down her arm to clasp her own hand, feeling her faint quiver. "Your hiccups are gone," he added.

She hesitated, then smiled up at him, open, unwary. "Yes."

He caught his breath at the natural sensuousness of her smile. He doubted she knew what a siren she could be, and chuckled once more.

"You're doing it again," she said, her expression becoming puzzled. "Laughing at nothing."

"Genetic weakness," he said softly, mimicking her. "Mother had it."

Fiery red, she turned away in a valiant attempt to ignore him. Given the opportunity, Hawk avidly studied her. She glittered with fire and anger, and the combination was electric, tantalizing. She was quite unaware of her beauty, and simply by standing near him, she made his libido kick in, his blood pound. And she'd been able to do that almost from the first moment of their meeting. His mind rebelled against that. Years of being in control had given him the strong impression that it would always be that way. One woman, no matter how gorgeous, couldn't change that. Yet even as he studied her again, looking for some flaw that would repel him, his body and spirit reacted ever more strongly to her. He fought the arousal.

Bahira returned his stare, royally annoyed with herself for letting him affect her. She figured it must have taken him years of practice to refine his sexual power. How many women had he used it on? Her rampant curiosity about him further irritated her, and she shut her mind against all those titillating questions. It was to little avail though. He exerted a powerful attraction, and she had to struggle against its pull. Her heart turned over every time he looked at her. Her knees wobbled whenever he touched her. Her eyes enjoyed staring at him, and no amount of willpower could turn her gaze away. It was as though her body was rebelling against her mind.

No! No! she thought desperately. Not ever, not for one minute, would she succumb to his charm. She'd just pull herself together and shove him into the bottom drawer of her mind. She could do that. All it would take was the same self-control, determination, and grit that had carried her through the past several years. Now they could dig Hawk Dyhart out of her mind and make her forget him. He could just test his bedroom skills on someone else.

Firm of purpose, she tilted her chin up and stared straight into his eyes. Forgetting about the guests milling around the garden area in front of the hotel, she let the ire build until it smoked out of her.

"Now you listen here, Mr. Dyhart. I won't take any of your cutesy remarks or veiled insults. Nor will I allow you to haul me along like old laundry. I'm in charge of this tour. I work for a living and am beholden to no one. I'm Yankee born and tough as old boots if I have to be, and I'm not impressed with your wealth or status. So, watch it." So intent was she in getting her message across, she poked him in the chest for emphasis.

Amusement dancing in his eyes, he nodded toward the small group of interested observers. "I get it. So do they."

Bahira turned, gasped, then looked back at him, her expression resigned. "I did it again," she muttered, then flinched when he had the nerve to laugh out loud.

Lord, no, she thought. She couldn't have

poked him in the chest. That wasn't her style. Manners and decorum had been drummed into her at Madame Ridaut's Academy for Young Women in Switzerland. She would never do anything so rude. Closing her eyes for a moment, she wished she were back in L.A. . . . or Morocco . . . or even outer Mongolia. Anywhere but there. Her mind was obviously going. Could she explain that to Hawk Dyhart? The man was a trickster, a sleight-of-hand artist. That had to be it. He brought out the worst in her with his—his underhanded ways. He'd seduced her into bad manners. What other tricks did he have up his sleeve?

She risked a glance at the bystanders. They were eyeing her expectantly.

"Now see what you've done," Hawk whispered to her. "They're waiting for more. They want Act Two."

"Don't be ridiculous," she hissed back, then tried to smile reassuringly. "Excuse us," she said to the guests. "Misunderstanding." Face flaming, she turned away. What else would she do to endanger her position at the Grand Bajian?

"Has your dentist ever told you," Hawk asked pleasantly as the other guests lost interest in them, "that grinding your teeth like that is bad for them?"

"No." Don't look at him! Bahira warned herself. If she did, his sexuality would ensnare her again, and heaven only knew what she would say. Still, as he remained silent, she couldn't resist glancing at him.

He was staring at her! Hotly. Hungrily. As if he wanted to drag her back to his condominium.

"The bus," she managed to say.

The croaking desperation in Bahira's voice told Hawk more clearly than words that she felt the potent sensuality simmering between them. His concentration was on her fully. Each nuance in look and voice telegraphed messages to him about the entrancing Bahira Massoud. She was vital, warm, eager, exciting. She had a temper, and more spirit than ten people put together. She was the most intriguing woman he'd ever met.

"Why are you staring at me, Mr. Dyhart?" she asked, obviously rallying herself.

"Hawk. Was I doing that?"

"Yes."

"Maybe it's because you're lovely." He was fascinated by the play of emotions over her face. She had the dauntless air of a Trojan in a woman's beautiful body.

"I'm your guide," she said hoarsely.

"So you are." Though a veritable tiger within, he mused, she looked like she'd be more at home in a seraglio.

"You're still staring."

"Maybe I'm losing my mind."

"Not on my tour," she sputtered.

Delight bubbled up in him. Throwing his head back he let it loose in a laugh more full and happy than any he remembered. When was the last time he'd enjoyed someone's company so much? All his adult years he'd sought anonym-

ity, assiduously avoiding the spotlight. Two
minutes with Bahira and she'd managed to
focus all sorts of attention on him. Laughter
rolled out of him.

Bahira blinked and stepped back, eyeing him
suspiciously. "What's so funny now?" she asked.
Cognizant of the people still milling around, she
lowered her voice. "You'd better not be laughing
at me."

"Who else?" he said, chuckling. "You're obviously the comic relief around here. Oww. That's
my shin." Hawk glared at her.

She stared at him, as nonplussed by his laughter as she was by the strange wildness building
inside her. The whole situation was insane, yet
she was feeling a reckless disregard for her repu-
tation, her position at the hotel. Years of caution
and careful planning were in danger of melting
away. Common sense was ready to fly out the
window. And *he* was doing it. Hawk Dyhart!

He took her hand. She stiffened, but didn't
pull free. She couldn't seem to muster her earlier
irritation with him. For a flashing moment all
the previous warmth of her younger life washed
over her, the laughter, the carefree days, the
high hopes. Only with Hawk she felt so much
more than simple warmth. She felt the intensity
of the sun itself.

They were silent as he led her to the sidewalk.
To the left the narrow main road led into Bridgetown; to the right it wound around the top of the
island.

"I don't see the bus," she remarked.

"Maybe that's it," he said, gesturing to the left.

Down the block was a small terminal, and Bahira saw a bus edging out of it and heading toward them. The late-day sun glared off the windshield, and she couldn't identify the driver.

No name had been listed in the reservation book, which happened sometimes when it was busy and changes were constantly being made. She squinted against the reflection of the sun, then sighed in recognition and resignation when the ancient bus halted in front of them and the beaming driver opened the door. They'd got the worst driver of the lot.

"We're going with Harry Banetree," she said to Hawk, and tried to smile. No sense trying to explaining to Hawk about Harry. Words couldn't define him.

Hawk nodded. "It doesn't matter who it is as long as he knows our itinerary. We're going to have a little private tour, then we'll eat at La Bagatelle. I've heard the food's very good there."

"You'll get more than you bargained for with Harry," Bahira muttered. She toyed with the idea of suggesting she walk to La Bagatelle and Hawk and Harry could take their own tour, but she knew she couldn't do that. Her services as tour guide had been paid for. She rolled her eyes as the rosy-nosed Harry made a sweeping bow and bade her enter his rattletrap vehicle.

Before she could move, Hawk put his two hands on her waist and lifted her up the high step into the bus.

Her blood thundered through her at his

touch. He'd lifted her as though she were a feather, she thought. His long, strong fingers had held her so intimately— Stop it, Bahira! she ordered herself. She wouldn't think about Hawk, except as a client. She'd forget his hands, his narrow hips, his wide shoulders. . . . Damn. She gave up the struggle and gestured for him to take a seat. She remained standing in the aisle, facing him, a smile pinned to her lips.

"Just a short distance from here," she began, "is the—" As she lifted her hand to point, Harry threw the bus into gear, knocking her against the seats. With a grinding of the gearshift and to the accompaniment of several blaring horns, Harry pulled out onto the narrow road. Clutching the back of a seat, Bahira glared at Hawk, who was still standing. His legs apart and braced against the swaying of the bus, he grinned at her. Ignoring him, she turned and switched her scowl to the driver's back. "Harry! For heaven's sake."

"And how are you this foine evening, Bahira, my girl?" Harry asked her over his shoulder. His red hair stood up in spikes all over his head. His determination to be a punk rocker was slightly ludicrous since Harry was on the downside of forty.

"I'm fine, Harry. Slow down." Straightening her clothing, she sat down, then shifted over on the seat as Hawk moved beside her. Her prepared speech went right out the window as his nearness made her whole being quiver like soft gelatin. "We should have invited some other guests," she said, staring straight ahead. "It's a shame to waste all this space."

"What's first on the tour?" Hawk asked. He watched her swallow, and felt a strong urge to kiss her throat. The croaky sound of her voice sent shivers up and down his spine. He tried to ignore the wild feelings Bahira Massoud engendered in him, but it was impossible.

Women were important to him, and had been since he was a teenager. Some of them he'd wanted badly, but he'd always managed to keep a clear perspective on his relationships. With Bahira, though, his self-confidence was on half-power, his self-assurance somewhat dented. Why was he so intense about her?

"Quite a few famous people live on Barbados," she said, bringing his attention back to the private tour he'd paid dearly for.

"Will we see any of their homes?" he asked, though he couldn't have cared less. Simply being with Bahira was the important thing. He was feeling a strange urgency to know everything about her.

He glanced at the driver and caught Harry watching them in the rearview mirror. Too bad he couldn't be totally alone with her. Looking back at Bahira, he was surprised to see she was blushing. "Do I make you uncomfortable?" he asked.

"Maybe. I mean, no," she stammered. "It's just I can't recall any famous person. And it's part of my spiel." She smiled weakly when he threw back his head and laughed. "It's not that funny."

"It is." He stretched his arm across the back of the seat, his fingers mere millimeters from her shoulder. She hadn't even noticed he'd been staring at her. Good. "Actually, I'd just as soon look at nature, rather than people's homes."

She glanced at him, frowning for a moment, then she smiled tentatively. "Thanks. That's kind of you."

"Don't be so surprised. I once passed a dog and didn't kick it." Blood thrummed through him when a dimple flashed at the corner of her mouth. She seemed totally unaware that she was a real heartbreaker when she did that. She'd got under his skin, both annoying and titillating him. How the hell had she managed that so quickly?

"You're frowning," she said resignedly. "I know I'm a lousy tour guide tonight."

"It's not that at all," he murmured. On impulse he leaned closer and kissed her cheek.

Startled, she stared at him. "It's just a tour," she said in strangled voice. "No side dishes."

Amusement rose in him. He sternly tamped it down. "That's what I thought."

"I don't want you to get ideas."

Too late, Bahira Massoud, he thought, but only said mildly, "Of course."

Unwarranted disappointment spread through Bahira, and she turned away from him, looking out the window blindly. "There are many hills in Barbados," she said, struggling to maintain her tour-guide role. She doubted she would succeed. Right now, her brain needed reupholstering. How could she be so foolish to want a man like Hawk Dyhart?

Harry suddenly yanked the bus into a right turn, onto an even-narrower road. Hawk was thrown against Bahira, knocking her shoulder against the window. She gasped at the sudden impact.

"Dammit, Harry," Hawk exclaimed. "Ease up. Are you all right, Bahira?"

She nodded. Hawk began to massage her bare shoulder, sending her world spinning. "I'm fine," she managed to say.

"We just passed Claudette Colbert's home, Bahira," Harry said meaningfully, glancing at her in the rearview mirror again.

"There it is," Bahira breathed, jerking her thumb over her shoulder, but not looking away from Hawk.

"Amazing," he said, smiling into her eyes.

"Well, it is," Harry grumbled, revving up the bus and speeding past the landmark.

Hawk tightened his arm around her shoulder, pulling her against him. "There. Maybe we can prevent a few bruises. All right?"

Bahira could only nod. Her body felt waxy-soft and her breath came in short gasps. Her eyes wouldn't focus on the scenery jouncing past.

"Bahira!" Harry called. "Mention the seashell house. There it goes. I'm supposed to be the driver," he added huffily. He made another almost ninety degree turn, then accelerated over a tooth-rattling bump.

The resulting bounce of the bus loosened

Hawk's hold on Bahira, and she ended up half on his lap.

"This is sight-seeing Harry Banetree—style," she said, wondering if Hawk would have both her and Harry fired for this fiasco. She tried to scramble off Hawk's lap, but he groaned and reflexively tightened his arms around her. She could feel him harden beneath her, and her own body felt as though it were melting. The sudden softening wetness in her lower body was threatening to her. Where was her self-control? She could feel his body moving beneath her, going from muscular to steellike. She closed her eyes and willed herself not to react. Too late. Of its own volition her body swayed against him.

This wasn't supposed to happen! she screamed silently. She'd orchestrated her life, her projections for the future, where she'd go and how she'd get there. It had been like climbing an ice mountain: go up three feet, slip back two. Eventually, she'd got a toehold, and she wouldn't slide back now. And Hawk Dyhart would be a monumental icy fall for her.

So he was handsome and rich. Those weren't necessary criteria for her. He did seem in charge of his reflexes and much of his sanity, but she could find that elsewhere. He was just a man, not the answer to her dreams. She could handle him. Handle him? Oh, Lord, what a thought.

Just as her imagination was about to run away with her, Harry stomped in the brakes. The sudden stop nearly sent his two passengers sliding to the floor.

"Sorry about that, folks," Harry said as he shut off the motor. "Got good brakes, thanks be to God." He tapped the quarter-keg next to his seat. "Time for refreshments. Then you can get out and see the monkey farm." He reached down and turned the nozzle on the side of the keg. A mahogany-colored liquid spilled into a Styrofoam cup. "Tea," he said, smiling. "Would you like some? Some call it Bajian punch. I calls it tea. It's good for what ails ya."

Hawk set Bahira onto the seat and stood up. "I could use some of that."

"That's the way, bucko." Harry filled another cup and handed it to Hawk.

Hawk took a hefty swallow, then his features contorted. Red flooded his face as a harsh cough erupted from his throat. "Damn, what is it?" Eyes watering, he stared into the cup.

"Tea," Bahira said, her mouth trembling with amusement. "Serves you right. The island punch is drained from carburetors, some say."

" 'Tain't so," Harry said indignantly. "It's pure. Me own mother drinks it."

Bahira looked askance at the driver. "You don't have a mother, Harry."

"I musta had. I'm born, ain't I?"

"I'll go and see the monkeys," Bahira said. "You can stay and recover, Mr. Dyhart."

"I'm coming with you," Hawk said hoarsely, setting down the cup.

"Ya might be better to finish it, boyo. Sometimes the stuff leaks through the cup. Melts it, ya might say."

"Eats it through is what he means," Bahira said dryly.

"No doubt," Hawk muttered. He glared at the cup, then at Harry, then quaffed the rest of the "tea." "Let's go," he said, barely repressing a shudder. "You can show me the monkeys." He coughed to clear the raspiness from his voice. He was damn sure Harry's "tea" had all but eroded his vocal cords.

"You'll be drunker than a brewer's pup if you try to keep up with Harry," Bahira told him as they exited the bus. "You might be now. I think your eyes just crossed."

"Did they really? I wouldn't worry about me. I can hold my liquor." He neglected to mention the fact that his mouth felt as though it were on fire.

"I hope you can." Turning her back on him, she walked toward the first of a series of enclosures. Sniffing and wrinkling her nose, she paused. "I can't say I ever like the smell of this place."

The combination of Harry's tea churning in his stomach and the pungent odor around him had Hawk rearing back and shaking his head. "I pass."

"Don't you want to see the monkeys?" Bahira asked, glancing back at him. He was massaging his stomach, and she smothered a laugh. Good old Harry. His "tea" could level anyone.

"No, thanks," he said. "There are other minor hells I'd choose first." His eyes narrowed as she couldn't quite hide her grin. "Enjoying yourself?

You have a strange sense of humor, Bahira Massoud."

"So I've been told." He really was a good sport, she thought. He could have railed at her about the "tea" about the monkey farm, which was rarely on the tour. But he was taking it in stride . . . unfortunately. She didn't want to like him.

Hawk smiled ruefully. "I think Harry's 'tea' melted my fillings." When she laughed, *he* almost melted. She'd got under his guard, and he had a suspicion she knew it. The thought discomfited him. He was drawn to her, sought her company, but he didn't like the sensation of being emotionally stripped, exposed, made vulnerable. Dumping Bahira in Harry's bus and whisking her back to the hotel would be the smart move. Even as he thought it, though, he knew he wouldn't do it.

"We'd better go," he said. "We have dinner reservations."

Bahira nodded, though at the moment she was concentrating more on the man himself than what he'd said. Hawk had a *savoir-faire* she admired, however grudgingly. He was handling the dilapidated bus, Harry's "tea," and the monkey farm with an aplomb that seemed inborn. On the other side of the coin, though, she knew he was not for her. They traveled different roads.

"Bahira?" he said, and his voice snapped her from her reverie. "I'd just as soon go. The smell really is awful, and I'm not very fond of caged animals."

She smiled. "I feel the same way, and I try not to come here often." She looked toward the cages. A monkey mother was cuddling her baby in one of the small, grimy pens. "You go ahead. I'll be right along."

"It doesn't help to watch them," he said. "You'll only feel worse." When she didn't answer but started walking toward the cages, he called after her, "Don't be too long."

"I won't. And watch yourself with Harry's keg. You'll end up swinging through the trees with the wild monkeys." She stopped in front of the cage with the mother and her baby. After looking over her shoulder at the departing Hawk, she whisked a nail file from her purse.

"This is crazy, you know," she muttered to the monkey as she twisted the file in the lock. "I could lose my job, and you probably wouldn't bail me out if I got arrested. Oh, damn, this will never—"

The click of the lock sounded like a cannon boom. Glancing left and right, she removed the lock and opened the cage door. "Go on now. Run. Take your baby and scoot."

The animal stared at Bahira for a moment, then picked up a piece of unrecognizable dried fruit and munched on it.

"Great, now you eat. Move, will you, toots?" Bahira ordered the monkey.

As though the message had gone around the compound, the other monkeys began to hoot and squeal. Bahira felt as though she were on a firing line.

"Scoot, will you?" She reached into the cage. The monkey screamed and slapped at her hand. Then, quicker than the eye could watch, she raced from the cage, her baby clutched to her middle. Touching the ground only for a moment, she swung up to the top of the open-sided building housing the cages, scuttled across it, and leaped into an overhanging tree.

"Keep low and quiet," Bahira warned softly. Then she closed the cage, slipping the lock through the hasp but not fastening it. Smiling, she headed back to the bus.

Hawk was leaning over in the doorway as though he were about to come down the steps. "What were you doing?" he asked when he saw her. "I was just coming back for you. I thought you might've passed out from the stench."

"I was just . . . communing with nature."

He frowned at her and at the monkey farm, then took her arm and helped her into the bus. "Let's get out of here, Harry. Make it quick."

"Yes, fast," Bahira murmured, glancing out the window.

Harry started the bus with a roar, ground the gears as always, and lurched out of his space, the wheels throwing up stones.

"Harry," Hawk said, pointing out the window, "a man's waving at you. Maybe he wants to tell you something."

Bahira slid lower in her seat.

"Oh? That's old Cyril. Nice chap." Against all

safety rules, Harry opened his door, but didn't stop. "Right you are, Cyril. Can't stop. Schedule!" Harry bellowed over the coughing roar of the engine. Cyril continued to wave his arms frantically as Harry shut the door and sped down the driveway. "Nice feller, but a bit of a tippler, so they say. Must have been dippin' deep. I think he thought we had one of his monkeys."

Hawk turned to Bahira, who smiled weakly. "I thought he said something about turning the monkeys loose," he said, "Know anything about that?"

"I wouldn't do anything to jeopardize my job, would I?" she said loftily.

He laughed. "You little devil."

"I don't know what you mean. Maybe you should tell Harry to hurry. We don't want to be late for the reservation at La Bagatelle."

Still grinning, Hawk glanced at his watch. "We have forty-five minutes."

"Still, we won't have time to stop at Sam Lord's Castle if you want to see the Caves of the Winds," she said, then paused. "It'll be better than the monkey farm," she added mischievously. At the pained expression on his face, she burst out laughing.

Harry grinned at them in the rearview mirror and took a healthy gulp of "tea." "Had a foine time, did ya? You'll be bragging to your friends about the loo-vely experience, I've no doubt."

"I think you'd better lay off that stuff for the rest of the trip, Harry," Hawk said firmly. He glanced at the lethal keg, then massaged his temples.

"Getting to you?" Bahira bit her lip to keep from laughing.

"A bit," he said brusquely.

Harry shook his head. "I can't believe you'd worry about me tea. It's wondrous good for you. Efficacious, as they say. No one in my family has ever had bowel rot," he pronounced solemnly.

Bahira couldn't control her laughter. "How's your bowel rot these days, Mr. Dyhart?"

Hawk sent her a mock frown, then slipped his arm around her bare shoulders again, drawing her close. Her smile was magic. Just for this one night, he'd allow that magic to take control.

Bahira relaxed against him, realizing with a little shock that she hadn't felt this happy in ages. Hawk was warm and exciting. Even as she listened to the voice deep inside her warning her away from him, she was irresistibly drawn to him. She wouldn't listen to admonitions this time, for this one short evening. There would be enough of those after he'd left Barbados. What was the harm in enjoying this moment in time?

She sighed. She'd had more than enough of caution and prudence, of husbanding resources and funds. The end result had often been loneliness. Not that she'd deliberately cut herself off from her friends, but it had happened anyway to an extent. She'd needed to work hard, keep her nose to the grindstone, and there had been times she was grindingly lonely. As she pondered Hawk's departure a few days hence, that loneliness engulfed her once more. He'd managed to pierce all her hard-built barriers.

If the damage was already done, then, she rationalized, why not have an evening of pure, unadulterated fun?

Hawk noticed her introspection, her retreat into her mind. He didn't like being shut off from her, and he liked even less the sadness he saw in her eyes. "It's not polite," he said lazily, "to laugh at someone who's in pain." He watched as she focused on him, then a smile slowly curved her mouth.

"I told you about Harry's tea," she said.

"So you did." Whatever specter had appeared in her mind seemed to have dissipated, and she was once more at ease. It pleased him that he'd been able to distract her. Impulsively, he leaned over and kissed the corner of her mouth.

"Why did you do that?" she asked breathlessly.

"I don't know. Maybe because you have a very tempting mouth, Bahira Massoud." He felt reckless, wild, and he doubted he could blame Harry's damn tea.

"Oh." She stared at him, at his eyes, his mouth. "Harry's tea is talking," she said shakily.

"Maybe." He leaned closer, his lips just grazing hers.

Bahira felt propelled to him, though she didn't move. She reeled with the sexual reaction, and with the sure sensation she must be losing her mind. She was caught in a whirl of emotion.

Their mouths touched again, then joined, connected, though their hands were still, bodies free. It was enough. They spun into the vortex, the spark from their lips firing them beyond sensual love and into the strange fantasy of initial passion that no one can explain. Bahira was on the verge of drowning in rivers of alien feeling, when Harry's hearty voice tore them apart.

"Well, look at that ocean, will ya? Looks like a good beer with a foine head on it, wouldn't you say?" He frowned at them in the rearview mirror. "Is Bahira describing all our wonders to ya, sir?"

"She is." Hawk turned and squinted at the beaming driver, who had thrown his arms wide to encompass their expansive view of the Atlantic Ocean. Hawk barely noticed, though. He was shaken, his well-ordered emotional center off balance, and all because of one beautiful woman.

"My life's in order," he heard her whisper, as if she were denying that what they had just shared had affected her at all.

He tightened his arm around her shoulders and looked back at her. "I thought mine was too," he said softly, answering her quivering attempt at self-assurance. "You shivered. Are you cold? Here, let me raise that window."

"No, no, I'm fine. We need the air," she said, and smiled weakly.

The bus lurched up a hill and around another corner, revealing one more wild and wonderful view of the crashing Atlantic Ocean. Hawk still didn't notice. All of his attention was fixed on

Bahira. He'd seen how white she'd become after he'd kissed her. Had she hated it? No. He'd felt her response: her heat had answered his. Then why did she seem so scared? He stared down at her, and her tremulous smile made him catch his breath.

The bus lumbered around one last hairpin turn, spitting up pebbles and dirt. The almost-bald tires caused the bus to fishtail when Harry braked.

"Here we are," he announced triumphantly, not seeming to notice that the front of the bus teetered very close to the edge of the precipice. "The Cave of the Winds. You'll like it. It's wondrous. Have a care, though. We've lost a few tourists here. *Whoops* on that slippery stone floor, and into the ocean they go." He swept his hands toward the Atlantic and laughed merrily. "That's me little joke. Everybody out."

"All two of us," Bahira muttered. Hawk chuckled as he followed her down the aisle. "This you'll like," she added. "It's downright lethal for swimming, but the view is great."

As soon as they were out of the bus, she put a couple of feet of distance between them and began her spiel on the Cave of the Winds.

Hawk shoved his hands in his pockets, allowing her to keep him at arm's length. Her nervousness was endearing, and he watched her more than the scenery as they approached the wide steps leading down to the caves. Her pareau showed off her curves and sweet muscles, and he ached to hold her again. That thought made his blood pressure rise in pleasurable fashion.

Bahira glanced at him sideways and saw his smile. What was he thinking? she wondered. Her heart was still thumping wildly from that kiss—and it had been the merest touch.

She rushed her words, tumbling over the explanations of the underground chambers as they descended the slippery steps into the caves. The noise level from the ocean battering the rocky promontory coupled with the roar of the winds blasting through the huge openings to the sea and sky, rendered conversation all but impossible. Hand gestures and head movements were more efficient. They removed their shoes and carried them.

High above the ocean, they walked closer to one of the mammoth openings, isolated in sound and space. As the wind whipped through the blow holes, booming, crying, and howling, Hawk and Bahira gazed at each other wordlessly.

She didn't know when he'd taken her hand, or even if she'd taken his, but when he pulled her in front of him, his body shielding hers, she didn't resist. His body protected her. She felt warm, unafraid, loath to leave his arms.

Hawk could feel her heart pounding, and he tightened his hold, wanting her touch, needing it. He rubbed his face in her hair, then kissed it gently. She turned her face to him, and he let his lips move over it, his breath caressing her.

When other tourists arrived, the mood was

broken. Bahira moved free of Hawk, feeling sheepish, disappointed, disoriented. When she would have rushed around him, back toward the steps, he stopped her, taking her hand again. His easy smile made her blood boil. If she hadn't felt his heart thundering against her back, she would have thought he'd been totally unaffected. He was so cool, so contained. He had too damn much power!

"We should leave," she said huskily. "Dinner reservation."

"Right."

A sudden splash of water cascaded near them. She pressed closer to him to escape the wetness—and felt his lips caress her ear! Then he abruptly released her as the other tourists moved closer, jostling for a view of the ocean from the cave.

The precious bubble of time was burst.

"Let's go," Hawk said brusquely, taking hold of her arm. He didn't mean to be so harsh, but his response to her shocked him. Powerful sensations he'd never experienced before had coursed through him when he held her, and he could feel the backwash of them still. He quickly led her up the wide exit stairs of the caverns.

"Bajian Tours," she said stiltedly, "hoped you enjoyed seeing the Cave—"

"I did," he interrupted.

She looked up at him. "So did I," she said softly.

He paused and smiled at her, and was pleased when she smiled back. "You may tell your employers I liked the tour very much. Actually, I'll tell them myself." She was so lovely, he mused. Her green eyes, creamy skin, and black hair were an exotic combination that titillated his sense of beauty and made his libido leap to life. "Of course," he added dryly, "that's assuming I survive Harry's tea."

Laughing, she shook her head. "Never assume."

Her amusement cascaded over him, making his pulse race, his blood gallop through his veins. Bahira Massoud was an enchantress. He pulled her close to him and touched her hair.

"You look like a little girl with your hair flying free about your face that way." He caught her hand when she started to push some strands back from her face. "Don't touch it. You look wonderful. . . ." He gazed down at her, smiling. "Carrying your shoes after wading in those pools knocks your tour-guide sophistication all to hell. You look like a teenager, Bahira."

"I'm—"

He touched her lips with one fingers, silencing her. "I don't care if you're a hundred, you look adorable." Knowing full well it was a fool's move, he kissed her, his mouth slanting over hers, parting her lips. His body responded explosively and immediately. Want streamed through him. He could have made love to her right there on the slick stone steps. Shock, passion, and delight melted into a desire so strong, it shook him to his toes. He, who'd given and taken so much in relationships, felt unfledged, untried, as he was deluged by erotic sensations.

Tongue dueled with tongue. Hands rose and settled at shoulders and waist. Fingers touched, explored. Bodies inched closer until thighs met and the world fell away. They were fused. One. Time stood still.

Bahira heard all the alarm bells clanging in some distant part of her mind. Her body and spirit didn't listen. Alive and joyous, she gave him back kiss for kiss. Passion drowned out prudence. Later she'd have ample time for regret. Now was time for joy. Until Hawk kissed her, she hadn't thought there was much missing from her life. She hadn't known she longed for it, longed for him, that he could fill a giant hole in her existence. Could she truly be satisfied with a moment in time?

Three

Dinner was tense. Though it was not often included, dinner at La Bagatelle could be part of a tour—for an exorbitant fee. The tour guide was then expected to extol the merits of the restaurant. Bahira would open her mouth to do just that, Hawk would look at her with his piercing leonine eyes, and her mind would go blank.

"Yes?" Hawk asked her at one point. "Did you want to say something, Bahira?"

"Did I mention that the restaurant was featured on television?" she said automatically, intrigued to realize his eyebrows were the exact shade of his hair.

"Twice," he said gently.

"There's more," she muttered. "I know there is. Maybe it'll come back to me."

"Do you often suffer lapses of memory?" Hawk

asked. He thought her exquisite. Her expressions went from laughter to sadness, and covered everything in between. Her mouth was beautifully shaped.

"I don't know," she said limply. "I can't recall."

"Interesting." As he took a bite of his platter-sized lobster tail from Grenada, he tried to remember the last time he'd enjoyed himself so much. Bahira was an enchanting blend of sophistication and naiveté, and she pulled him like a magnet.

Bahira scowled at Hawk, then lapsed into silence, cutting and eating her own lobster and trying to make her brain function. It was all his fault, she decided. She was a solid, responsible thirty-year-old woman with her life in control. Only a Rasputinlike person could have turned her brain to mush. He shouldn't have kissed her. She shouldn't have responded. She attacked her lobster tail, slicing off another chunk of the luscious meat, although it tasted like sawdust in her mouth.

After finishing his meal, Hawk sat back, studying her as he dabbed his mouth with his napkin. "Would you like a sweet?"

She shook her head.

"Then shall we dance?"

She shook her head again. Being held in his arms and, doubtlessly, making a fool of herself again, was not high on her list of things to do. Hawk was a dangerous man. She was certain he scooped up women like the lobstermen of Grenada scooped up their catch. She had no intention of being one of his juicy morsels. Besides, it had taken her too long to come to terms with the loneliness, the uncertainty, the sense of isolation, that had come right on the heels of her family's financial crisis. She'd had enough of fragmenting relationships in her life. To court more would be masochistic.

Hawk cocked an eyebrow at the waiter, gave an order, and in moments a bottle of rare cognac and two glasses sat at his elbow. Bahira shook her head in refusal, and Hawk gestured for the waiter to pour his. He twirled the brandy snifter in his hand, watching her closely. She was dwelling on something unpalatable. His guess was that it was something long-standing, and it was causing her to distance herself from him. He didn't like that. He wanted her back.

"Harry told me," he began idly, "that he was a relative of Sam Lord, the famous Barbadian pirate."

Bahira stared at him uncomprehendingly for a moment, then she shook her head. "That's a bouncer, and Harry knows it, but he persists in the lie anyway. Harry's stories are as potent as his tea."

"Formidable," Hawk murmured, noting the effort she made to bring her concentration back to him. He admired her fortitude . . . and was irritated at her ability to lose her focus on him so easily. Since he'd never pictured himself as a man who suffered from a delicate ego, he was also irritated with himself.

"Yes," she said, finally looking directly at him. "One wonders what Harry will concoct next."

Hawk had always enjoyed eye contact, the silent sexual jousting between men and women. Normally, it titillated him, but Bahira's look fully aroused him, even though he saw concern in her eyes. Was she worrying about their time in the caves? "A kiss isn't the end of the world, Bahira," he said softly, though he knew that was a lie. His whole damn life had gone into upheaval in a matter of hours. It was as though he'd lived a lifetime since he'd got on Harry's bus with her.

Startled, Bahira jerked in her chair and stared at him, not understanding his meaning for a few moments. Then she realized he was thinking of their torrid embrace in the caves. Embarrassment was dissipated by anger. "Quite true. Would it quite put you off stride if I told you I was thinking of something else?"

"I'd be devastated," he said mildly.

Not by word or gesture did he demonstrate anger. Yet, at that moment, Bahira knew he was simmering with it. She studied him. Just how many layers were there to Hawk Dyhart?

His indolent posture didn't fool her. It irked him more to know she hadn't dwelt on their kiss. But why would it matter to him? She knew he considered her just another conquest, maybe an easy one at that. His crooked smile was wreaking havoc with her breathing. When he cocked his head and looked at her inquiringly, she had the strange feeling there might be a bit of lettuce stuck between her teeth.

"Something wrong?" Her hand fluttered near her mouth.

"I'd like to dance, Bahira," he said.

It wasn't lettuce! Relieved, she jumped to her feet. "Good idea."

"You have chameleon responses," Hawk murmured. Her surprised look told him she'd forgotten he'd asked her to dance just minutes ago. Damn! He was going to know what person or thing consumed her interest. He didn't like to be shunted to one side in her thoughts. "After you," he said, rising. He watched the sweet undulation of her hips as she preceded him to the dance floor, realizing anew how totally unconscious she was of her sensuousness. He saw the piercing glances and double takes the other male diners gave her, and his hands curled into fists. He had to give the other men credit for good taste, though. Her slim, curvy body, wrapped in the pareau, was about as sweetly sexy as anything he'd ever seen.

When Bahira reached the dance floor, she turned into his arms, and she knew, at once, that dancing with him was a grave error. Breath left her body. Heat suffused her shoulders, arms, and neck. Her legs trembled.

Hawk must have felt her indecision, for he frowned at her. "Don't you like the rhythm?"

"I love steel bands." When his eyes narrowed as though he were trying to read her mind, she managed to smile. Awareness softened his hard mouth. He had read her mind! Panic had her tucking her head under his chin. That was another mistake. His elusive after-shave and the wonderful male aura of him had her reeling.

"I like steel bands myself," he said, pulling her close as he swayed to the soft beguine beat.

Wave after wave of sensation beat through her, as though the throbbing of the drums were a tattoo in her blood. She was drowning in hot emotion, and she couldn't swim away.

Pounding sexuality swept through Hawk's body. All the catchy innuendos that had been part of his repartee with women deserted him completely. He simply held Bahira tight and closed his eyes, letting the music and the potent feelings roll over him.

When the music stopped, they stepped back awkwardly, looking at the other dancers, and not at each other.

Hawk felt like a fool. For the first time in his life he was tongue-tied. Words were like concrete blocks in his mind, cumbersome, unwieldy.

Bahira ran a list of inanitites through her mind. Nothing seemed right. "It's getting late," she finally said. "I have the early shift in the morning."

"Of course."

Back at the table, Hawk signaled for the waiter. He paid the bill with a platinum credit card, then escorted Bahira to the door. "You're very quiet," he said. Was she thinking of their time in the caves? When they'd danced? Not about them at all?

Bahira tried to smile. "It's just that I have a long day tomorrow." And he would be merely a guest tomorrow. When she saw him, she'd smile politely. Maybe he'd smile back.

He took her hand. "Bahira, did you know you haven't hiccuped since we were in the caves?"

Trust him to remind her of when she'd all but thrown herself into his arms, she thought sourly.

"Hiccups don't last that long," she said, trying to pull her hand free. If he kept hold of her, the hiccups would probably come back.

"I guess not," he said, and released her hand.

They'd parted from Harry at the end of the tour, so it was necessary to call a cab for the return to the Grand Bajian. It wasn't a long drive, but, to Bahira, it took forever. She was relieved, at least, that Eldo, Dandy's cousin, was driving. He kept up a running commentary until they reached the hotel.

Bahira waved good-bye to Eldo; then, as she turned toward the hotel, she caught her heel in one of the flagstones.

Hawk grabbed her around the shoulders, steadying her. The feel of her satiny skin burned through him. His annoyance with her, fed by her seeming indifference to him, melted away. He gently rubbed her soft skin and leaned close, his mouth near her ear. "Are you all right?" he whispered.

"Thank you, yes," she gasped, flushing.

He curled his fingers through hers and led her along the winding path, past the open-air lobby and skirting the small groups of people along the way. "I'll see to it you don't trip again," he said, and tightened his grip on her hand.

Hawk was shaken. He'd never felt such an overwhelming need for a woman, not even when he'd been a randy teenager. Maybe it was Barbados, maybe it was the food or Harry's tea. Whatever it was, he didn't want to say good night to Bahira Massoud.

At the foot of the outdoor staircase leading to the staff apartment, she turned to him, holding out her right hand. "There was no need for you to walk me here. But thank you, and good night, Mr. Dyhart."

"Hawk," he said softly. She'd avoided using his name all evening. When the dimple appeared at the corner of her mouth as she smiled fleetingly, his heart hammered against his ribs.

"Hawk." She looked up at him, then glanced away.

"You live on the first floor?" he asked.

She shook her head. "Third."

He turned her and started up the stairs.

"Really, there's no need . . ." The look on his face made her subside. He kept a hand loosely at her waist, as they climbed the narrow stairway, and it seemed to burn right through her clothing. At her door she turned again.

"Thank you for the—" She looked up at him and gasped. His mouth was centimeters from hers. "—wonderful evening," she finished slowly, mesmerized by his eyes, even as she berated herself. He hadn't been her date. Yet his eyes! They glittered sensually, and she felt lost in them. All her girlish dreams of the right man magically appearing in front of her were no longer fanciful longings. They were tangible, touchable, becoming solid right in front of her!

"It was more than wonderful," he murmured, bending nearer.

A door opened nearby. Light slanted across them. "That you, Bahira?" a woman called softly. "I need a blouse for tomorrow. Can you spare one?"

"Hell," Hawk muttered, grinding his teeth.

"Sure, Melda," Bahira answered. "I'll get it for you in a minute."

"Thanks." The door shut, the light disappeared.

Hawk scowled down at her, looking like a little boy whose favorite toy had been snatched away from him. Amusement bubbled within her. She tried to control it, but it tripped out of her, her laughter echoing softly down the hall.

Hawk continued to glare for a minute, but slowly his features changed, his fierce expression smoothed. "Why the hell are you laughing?" he asked, but he couldn't help grinning too.

"You. You could've scared Melda."

He tried to frown again, but couldn't hold on to it. He sighed instead. "For a small island, there sure are a hell of a lot of interruptions."

Bahira nodded and moved back from him. "I have to go in. I hope you enjoyed your tour."

"You know I did." He lifted her hand, turned it over, and placed a feathery kiss on her palm.

Bahira was flying. Breathing was an effort, and she had to concentrate on it before her chest burst. Her entire body was shaking—and he'd only kissed her hand!

"I'll see you tomorrow," he murmured.

"I have to work," she managed to say.

"I know." Hawk felt excited, energized, but a strange, lazy satisfaction was also coursing through him, as though he'd found something he'd once lost and badly needed. "Did I tell you that you look stunning in that pareau?"

Steady, girl, Bahira warned herself. He had to be a past master at seduction. No doubt he had truckloads of women. Dizzily, she stared up at him. "Thank you." As she struggled to hold on to her barriers, a part of her whispered, *Just one night. Take just one night with him.*

"Your eyes are dreamy," he said. "What are you thinking?"

"Ah . . . nothing much."

"Tomorrow."

She shook her head. "I'm working."

"Not all the time."

She smiled, but said nothing. Taking out her key, she unlocked her door. "Good night," she said over her shoulder.

"Good night, Bahira," he said, and just before she stepped inside, he kissed the top of her bare shoulder.

Bahira shut the door and pressed her back against it, willing her heart to stop thudding wildly. Finally, she pushed away from the door and walked toward her bedroom like an automaton. When she looked at her alarm clock, she was surprised to see it had only been minutes since she'd left Hawk, not eons.

Going to the closet, she took out one of her clean uniform blouses, then knocked on the wall. Returning to her door, she opened it and met Melda on the landing.

"You been drinking, Bahira?" Melda asked as she took the blouse. "You look a little off center. But hey, your date was something. He sure is no island man. I'd know it."

"He was the tour I took out tonight." Bahira tried to smile at the ebullient Melda, but Hawk seemed to have captured her mind and spirit. "I had Harry," she added, hoping to distract her friend.

Melda rolled her eyes. "Get down on your knees and thank your Maker you're still alive. But how come your 'tour' brought you home? You're supposed to leave the guests in the lobby."

"He insisted," Bahira said. "I have to get to bed, Melda. I'm tired, and I'm on the morning shift."

Melda looked as though she had a few more questions she'd like to ask, but she only nodded. "Sure. Thanks for the blouse."

Tired as Bahira was, sleep didn't come right away. Visions of Hawk Dyhart danced in her head. Smiling. Frowning. Laughing. Grimacing. His pained expression after his first sip of Harry's tea. His body pressed tight against hers as they swayed to beguine music. How he held his fork, his wineglass. The sweetness, the sophistication, the intelligence, the lazy hardness, all seeming to swim just below the surface of the man called Hawk. Bahira felt certain that his easygoing demeanor could quickly turn cold and tough.

A short time before the first glimmerings of the silvery predawn shivered on the horizon, her eyes closed and she slept.

On cue, as she'd done since being on her own, she awoke at six, squinting at the early sunlight streaming through the wooden lattices, over the window. Groaning, she knew she'd had some solid sleep, but nowhere near enough. Not willing to fight her body clock, she rose, felt around in the pale gold-gray light for her one-piece suit, and hauled herself into the bathroom. Brushing her teeth, throwing water on her face, and donning her suit took mere minutes. After pulling on a sweatshirt, beach slip-ons, and tossing a towel over her shoulder, she left her room and crept quietly down the stairs so that she wouldn't disturb the other sleepers in the staff complex.

The beach crews were out. Bahira knew Dandy would be among them, but she didn't seek out her friend. After her evening with Hawk—and the erotic dreams she'd had of him—she wasn't ready to face Dandy's scrutiny. It would be bad enough if he and his wife learned that Hawk had been the sole tourist on her tour the previous night. The conclusions they would doubtlessly jump to would be painfully accurate. She strode on toward her favorite stretch of beach, away from the more popular spots used by guests. Not that it mattered. The beach was all but deserted. Rays of sun sliced across the water like golden knives, making the rippling surface a gilt and diamond-studded crown for the sea world. After shucking her shirt and slip-ons, she pulled her cap and goggles into place and entered the Caribbean. She gasped at the initial coldness, then sighed at its silky feel. Diving forward, she sank down into the briny depths, the water's touch soothing, therapeutic. Swimming under water, she glanced at the wild and wondrous fish life swimming around her. When she ran out of breath, she surfaced.

"Good morning. You swim well."

The soft salutation had her spinning around, splashing water into her mouth. Hawk was in front of her, treading water easily. Sputtering, she struggled to stop coughing and to pull free of the muscular arm that encircled her. "I'm . . . all . . . right," she finally gasped.

Hawk pulled back when she wrenched off her goggles, noting how the sun reflecting on the water turned her green eyes a turquoise hue, and her skin a creamy, moist velvet. "Did you sleep well?" he asked. He hadn't. His aroused body had kept him awake much of the night, thoughts of Bahira continually prodding his libido. He could have found a woman to ease his desire, but he'd only wanted Bahira.

"Yes, thank you," she said politely, then slid her goggles back on and pushed free of him.

She began to swim parallel to the beach, and he kept pace with her. He was content to be at her side, shoving away the myriad mental warnings that Bahira Massoud was not for him. She would never understand the unspoken agreements he always had with the women he involved himself with; that is, no entanglements, easy come and easy go. Instinctively, he knew that Bahira would take very seriously any commitment she made. He couldn't figure out why, for the first time in his life, he found that attractive. He should get away from her. And that wouldn't be difficult, even on an island. She worked the front desk of the Grand Bajian. All he had to do was stay away from the lobby when she was on duty.

Yet despite Hawk's logical reasoning, he stayed at Bahira's side. When she dived, he mirrored her strokes and direction. When she climbed up onto a raft about a quarter of a mile from shore, he followed.

Bahira faced him, smiling uneasily. Hawk was a handsome man, she mused, all sharp angles and tough curves, narrow-waisted and slim-hipped, with long legs and a lean torso. She loved looking at him. "I can't stay," she said. "My shift . . ." Why was she explaining to him? She'd told him about her shift more than once the previous evening.

"I understand," Hawk said, though he hadn't been listening. He was too involved in looking at her. She was a strong swimmer, and he loved how that strength belied her faint air of delicacy. Her swimsuit clung to her, revealing the surprisingly lush curves of her slender body. Her eyes gleamed like emeralds in the early morning light, and drops of seawater glowed like pearls on her skin. And her legs . . . He could stare at them for hours. He knew he'd never seen a more sensuous, beautiful creature.

"You have long toes," he said absently, still staring at her.

"Guest or no guest, I won't stand still for an inventory, Mr. Dyhart," Bahira said tautly, angry that her nipples had puckered, her heart had thudded out of rhythm, at his look. Racing to the edge of the raft, she knifed outward in a racing dive. Hitting the water hard and kicking into speed, she opened up into a powerful crawl toward shore. It took her several seconds to realize Hawk was beside her, matching her stroke for stroke. And he was obviously not even swimming at full power. Furious at how she'd reacted to him, and how she was unable to put him out of her mind, she redoubled her efforts, crashing blindly toward the shore. Caught in her turbulent feelings, she didn't heed her direction. Before she realized it, she swam in over the wide coral bed. Confused, she allowed her feet to drop down before she spotted the sign printed for swimmers: DANGEROUS CORAL. She felt the first sting and knew she'd been cut.

"Wait." Hawk grabbed her around the middle, jerking her back to deeper water, even as he felt an astringent slice on his own foot. He swept her out with him, holding her just under the breasts.

"I'm all right," she exclaimed, fighting his grip.

"You will be." He knew she'd realized he wouldn't release her when her struggles subsided. Towing her parallel to the beach for a ways, he finally turned to shore just in front of his condo. With its sandy bottom, the area was devoid of the poisonous coral that could slash and infect.

Feathery helplessness washed over Bahira as he lifted her in his arms and strode toward his condo. She could feel the interested gazes of the few guests who'd begun to gather on the beach. But it was his arms, the strong thudding of his heart, the feel of his strong fingers on her back and legs that made the blood thunder through her.

Dandy came running up the beach, his straw hat flopping as though ready for takeoff. "What happened? Eel? Barracuda?" His voice was little more than a murmur as a consideration to the guests. Employees were adjured never to alarm the guests. Dandy held out his arms to take Bahira, but Hawk merely glared at him.

"Coral," he said shortly. "Get me some antibiotic soap and ointment, will you?" It felt so right to hold Bahira—she was light as cream in his arms—he didn't question his instant decision to treat her cut himself.

"Just put me—" she began.

"Shh. It's all right, Bahira," he said gently. "I'll

take care of things." He turned back to Dandy. "Bring them to my condo. Hurry."

"There's no need, really," she said. "How about your own—"

"I'll be right back," Dandy interrupted, then grinned as Bahira frowned at him. "You'll be okay," he whispered to her before running up the beach.

"You're making too much of a fuss," Bahira said. She could feel the stinging cut begin to throb, but she could deal with that. She was more shaken by the proximity to Hawk, the wonderful intimacy of his strong arms holding her. Her skin was tingling, a sensation she'd never felt before. . . .

Dammit! she thought. She was thirty years old, not some twittering teenager. She had to think of something else . . . anything else. As they neared the Coral Cottage, she tried to concentrate on that. It was the largest and most luxurious of the "Grand" condos. She'd never been inside, but she'd heard the maids describe it. When he carried her through the door, edging her around to keep from bumping her against the frame, Hawk's arms tightened. Her blood bucked into a nervous hot flood. Look at the fixtures, the ceiling, the furniture, she told herself. Study the plants, windows, rugs. Don't think about Hawk or his touch. Forget him.

"Trust you to have the best," she murmured, then bit her lip. She'd sounded bitchy. Whatever had happened to the cool renaissance woman she'd become? Hawk had trashed that image in mere seconds.

Hawk laughed. "I generally prefer the best, but I have been known to settle for less." He paused in the sitting room, loath to put her down on the striped cotton chaise longue. Unwittingly, his fingers stroked the supple skin of her thigh. When she stiffened, he grinned, awareness shooting through him. "Too tight?"

"Yes," she mumbled, not looking at him. "You can put me down now." When he didn't respond, she pushed against him.

"Relax, Bahira. We're not going anywhere until I get the antibiotics." He lowered her to the chaise, then knelt beside her, his face inches from hers. "It shouldn't take too long."

"I really don't have time." She stared at the gilded pendulum clock on the wall, glad to look at anything but Hawk Dyhart's eyes. "My shift starts in fifteen minutes."

"I'll take care of it." He reached past her to the phone on the table behind the chaise, his hand grazing her bare shoulder. After lifting the receiver, he dialed a two-digit number. "Why don't you take off that wet suit?" he suggested, glancing at her. "There's an afghan behind you." He smiled, then turned his back to her and spoke into the phone in a low voice.

Take off her suit! Bahira thought in astonishment. In front of him? Her mind and body turned to mush. If she could have risen, she would have run, but her legs felt all rubbery.

Closing her eyes, she took deep breaths. Get up, she told herself. Go.

"There," he said, hanging up the phone. "That's taken care of. You have the day off."

Her eyes flew open. "What! I can't do that. I'll lose too much money." Twisting around, she tried to get to the phone. "Another hour is all I need."

He stilled her hands. "No. You need that foot tended, then need to rest. Health is more important than money."

"Easy for you to say." She bit her lip. "Not that I'm not grateful for your care. I am. It's just that . . . I need my job."

Hawk saw the sudden haunted look in her eyes, the lacing of desperation. "What is it, Bahira? I can help." The words were out almost before he thought them, but he didn't want to call them back. She was as tart as a lemon, but she was also entrancing. His tour and dinner with her the night before had been one of the best evenings he'd ever spent. That alone was enough to make him curious about the exotic-looking Bahira Massoud. He gazed at her for a moment longer, then said, "I'll be right back."

He hurried into the small kitchen that looked out on the sitting room. He soaked a soft tea towel with liquid soap and hot water, then threw another towel over his arm. In no time he was back, kneeling in front of her. Picking up her foot, he began to swab the cut, back and forth, gently. He glanced up at her and was amused to see she was, once again, avoiding looking at him.

"You've been staring at that wall since our arrival," he said. "Either it's very interesting, or you don't want to look at me. Which is it?"

A reluctant smile trembled on her lips as her gaze slid back to him. "Well, it's a very intriguing pattern of stucco, and I like the pale coral hue," she said hesitantly, then added with a laugh, "Of course, you're not terribly boring."

He laughed with her, but he saw that shadows still haunted her eyes, and that bothered him. Why the shadows? And why did he care? "Stroking my ego, Bahira Massoud?"

"Does it need it?"

"It will need several bandages after you get through with me." Her laughter ran over his skin like sweet water.

"Oh, I think you'll survive." But would she? Bahira wondered. Hawk had already loosened the mortar in her defenses, got under her guard. And soon he'd be gone. They stared at each other for long seconds, and the only sound was the surf and the beach birds crying in the sky. Bahira swallowed and looked away first. "This is my first time in Coral Cottage. Tell me about it."

"The sitting room, kitchen, dining area, and lanai are on the first level," he said indifferently, not taking his eyes off her. "The master suite is the whole second floor."

She cleared her throat. "Very nice."

"Isn't it," he said silkily, swinging her foot around to rest on the chaise. As he laid a light afghan over it, the sea breeze fluttered through the open window, ruffling her hair. Irresistibly drawn to it, he ran his fingers through the drying strands.

Her head snapped at his touch, and waves of heavy, throbbing desire coursed through her. She shut her eyes. "Mr. Dyhart—"

"Hawk."

"Hawk." Swallowing uncomfortably, she pressed the injured area on the top of her foot. It was red and swollen, the cut all but hidden. It stung but didn't hurt. She shouldn't wait for Dandy, she thought. She could get antibiotic ointment herself. She had to get out of there. More than anything, she wished she had someone she could talk to about Hawk. What would Karim and her uncle say about him?

Hawk saw how her eyes darkened again, how she seemed to pull in on herself. "What is it, Bahira?"

She looked up at him. "I . . . uh, was thinking of my family. I haven't seen them in a long time."

"Oh? Why?" He had an irrepressible urge to know all about her.

She shrugged. "Many things, I suppose. They're in Los Angeles, I'm here. They're busy trying to make a living. . . . Her voice faltered and trailed off.

"I see." She was unhappy, he thought. Was she estranged from her family? When she started to rise, he gently held her back.

"I'm really fine," she said. "This isn't my first go-round with the coral. I can handle the rest."

"Fine, but since Dandy's bringing what you need, you might as well wait." He hesitated, staring at her. "You have unusual coloring," he whispered.

She stared back at him. "I resemble my father's family in my hair color," she said slowly. "But my features, height, eye color, are my mother's. She was born in the United States, of Irish parentage." She shook her head. "I should go. My work—"

"Dandy should be here soon. It's only been a few minutes."

She coughed nervously. "How about your cut? You should clean it too." Her eyes met his, and she felt giddy, dizzy. When his smile flashed, she almost melted clean through the chaise. She must be lacking vitamin A, she thought helplessly. She'd eat more pineapples, oranges, nuts, get on a strict regimen. She twisted her hands together to keep them from shaking.

"Do you want to tend to mine?" he asked, gazing intently at her. What was it about this woman that so attracted him? he wondered. She wouldn't look at him for more than a second at a time, and she was too quick off the mark, using her tongue like a scythe, but . . . But what? He'd met better-looking women, though maybe none with such exotic coloring. Then again, satin black hair and black-emerald eyes couldn't be that special. Her features, taken individually, certainly were not unique. Then why did she seem so one-of-a-kind?

He shook his head in irritation. He'd better

get back to the mainland, his job, and Netta Beaman. All at once, though, he couldn't recall what that haughty socialite looked like. Did Bahira Massoud have a boyfriend? He'd seen no evidence of one when he'd taken her home the previous night, but that didn't mean she wasn't involved with someone. Angry at his whirling thoughts, he roughly swiped at his own foot with the soapy cloth.

"Ouch!" she exclaimed. "Your way could hurt. Maybe I should do it." Unexpectedly, he agreed, and Bahira was startled when he sat back and propped his foot on the chaise.

Slowly, she swabbed the injury, her head down. He had a long foot with a high instep. She brushed the damp cloth back and forth, telling herself there was nothing erotic about his foot, and certainly nothing erotic about *washing* it. Why then was she finding the simple act so arousing?

Confused and distressed, she accidentally rubbed harder than she should have, and his foot recoiled instantly. She looked up at him. "I'm sorry. Did that hurt?"

"Yes . . . no," he muttered.

She frowned in puzzlement. "They do sting, but I'm almost done. How long are you staying in Barbados?" she went on, then groaned silently. Why had she asked him that? He was a guest. It was none of her business. She didn't want him thinking she cared if he stayed a minute or a month. "I'm sure you have to get back, to your business and . . . and other things." *Other women.* She dropped the towel and pushed away from him, feeling her face flush again.

"I'll stay as long as it takes," Hawk said cryptically. He eyed her slightly swollen foot and lifted it. He felt a quiver run through her, and his gaze lifted to her face. His smile was slow, aware, then he looked again at her foot. It was slender, beautifully shaped, with long toes. He examined the cut again, and she flinched. Lifting the foot to his mouth, he tenderly kissed the cut. Then his fingers feathered over all of her foot, stopping at her toes, massaging them, bending them up and down, treating each one with gentle absorption.

"All done," she said hoarsely.

He looked up at her, his eyes telling her he was far from done with her, then returned his attention to her foot. How could this be so damned erotic? he wondered. His heart thudded heavily against his breastbone. Bending over her, he again lifted her foot to his mouth. He allowed only the merest touch of his lips to her velvet skin, but it excited him wildly. "You can't go," he murmured. "Dandy's coming."

Bahira was losing oxygen. More than once, she lifted her hands to his hair, then tightened them into fists and pulled back without touching him. *Hawk.* Had she breathed his name? Or was it a sound in her soul? Her body wriggled in sensuous wonder. She was filled with an eagerness she couldn't define, an alien want she didn't dare name. All the wonderful sensations of their evening together flooded over her again.

Neither heard the outer door slam. "Mr. Dyhart?" Dandy called from the enclosed lanai. "I brought the antibiotics."

Both Bahira and Hawk looked up at the hotel attendant as though they'd never seen him before.

"The antibiotics?" Dandy held up the tube containing the medication, his sharp gaze flashing between them. "And I have antiseptic bandages too."

"Oh. Sure." Hawk nodded, his smile lopsided as he rose to his feet. "Thank you."

"Do you want me to take you back to your room, Bahira?" Dandy asked solicitously.

As she opened her mouth, Hawk spoke. "I'll take care of it. Thank you, Dandy. I'll call if I need anything else."

Silence.

Bahira eyed her friend wordlessly.

Dandy stared searchingly at her, then a small smile touched his mouth. "Just as you say, sir. Bahira, I'll see you later. Don't forget Althea expects you tonight. I can pick you up." He smiled. "She told you to bring a date. Right?"

"Yes." Bahira smiled weakly, ignoring Hawk's sharpened gaze. A voice inside her kept telling her to call Dandy back, but she didn't. She heard the screen door close. "I should go."

"Wait. I have to apply the medication." Hawk scowled at her. Why was she in such a hurry? "You have a free day."

"I need to work," she said firmly.

He smoothed in the cream, then applied a square bandage. "So you told me," he said tautly, annoyed that she was so damned anxious to get away from him. He helped her to her feet, keeping both hands at her waist. "I should carry you. Those slip-ons of yours could loosen the bandage and abrade the cut."

"Carry me all the way through the atrium?" Appalled, Bahira shook her head. She could imagine the looks on the guests' faces, her agog friends. "I can walk. No problem." And if she didn't get out of there that instant, she might ask him to kiss her other foot.

"Are you sure?" he asked as she edged toward the door.

"It's perfect. I should go. Don't forget your own foot."

"I'll call you later to find out how you are."

She started to turn to tell him not to bother, and the slight movement irritated the tender cut. She staggered.

In two strides he was beside her, taking hold of her arm. "I'm helping you to your room."

"No need. Really. I can get there on my own." If she didn't get away from him, she'd be throwing herself into his arms.

"I'll only walk you to your door."

His taut fingers telegraphed his anger with her. Bahira knew she was being ungracious, but she felt helpless against his sensual onslaught. How could he be unaware of the power he wielded? It was like an atom bomb.

He stroked her arm, catching hold of her

hand. His own hand was hard, and the feel of it sent waves of heat through her. She snatched her hand back and smiled weakly. "Gotta go. You've been very kind," she added stiltedly. Oh, Lord, she thought. She sounded like a school-marm.

"So I have," he answered sardonically, and took her arm, again to lead her from the condo and down the curving path to the main court-yard. "Slow enough for you?"

His solicitous tone didn't fool her. He was angry with her, and she couldn't blame him. But she had to get away from him. If she didn't, she'd explode.

"At least you don't have the hiccups," he said softly.

"Right." She swallowed in relief as they rounded the corner leading to the back of the staff complex.

Melda was coming down the stairs as they ascended, and her eyebrows rose expressively. "Hi, Bahira." She gave a thumbs-up sign.

"Hurt my foot," Bahira mumbled.

"Good idea," Melda said admiringly.

Hawk swallowed a chuckle, then put his arm around her waist and all but lifted her up the last flight of stairs. "Take an aspirin and try to sleep," he said when they reached her door.

"I will," she promised.

Returning to the Coral Cottage, Hawk prowled back and forth, then called his assistant in Chicago, catching him just before he left for the office. He gave the man a list of questions and instructions, then said. "Get back to me on this as soon as possible."

He was deeply immersed in his paperwork when his assistant called back two hours later with the information that he had located a Mohammar and Karim Massoud in Los Angeles. Hawk listened attentively, his face creasing into a frown. "All right," he said finally. "Find out everything you can about the takeover, and check the connection to Bahira Massoud." He replaced the receiver and drummed his fingers on the desk. "Are those two your family, Bahira Massoud?" he said aloud. After a moment's hesitation he called the desk to ask for some information and explained why he wanted it. Then he dialed a local number and introduced himself to the woman who answered.

Four

Bahira was amazed that she did nap. When she woke, she felt refreshed. She called the hotel manager, reassured him of her good health, and asked if he wanted her to come on for a few hours. When he said yes, she swallowed a sigh of relief that she would only lose three hours of work instead of eight. Racing through a quick shower and dressing at top speed, she was out the door and down the stairs, in record time, barely wincing at the slight sting in her injured foot. But every time she felt that sting, she thought of Hawk Dyhart.

Work was steady all afternoon, with little chance for a break. Hawk was at the edge of her mind all the while. Everyone who faced her had his voice, his laugh, his smile, that satirical twist of his mouth. No amount of work chased him away, and somehow she managed to keep from making too many mistakes.

As the day wore on, the throbbing in her foot worsened, and she propped it on a box behind the desk as often as possible. At the end of her shift she was relieved to see that Loula was uncharacteristically on time to replace her. She'd been weaker than she'd thought, and her foot now had a feverish pulsing that was a constant reminder of Hawk.

Favoring her foot, she hurried across the inner courtyard to the staff complex. Climbing the stairs hurt, and she winced more than once. She sighed when she reached the third-floor landing, and as soon as she was inside her apartment, she stripped off her clothes and headed for the bathroom. She turned the spigots on full and dumped a hefty amount of salts into the hot water.

Soaking in the foaming soft water was heaven, and she reveled in it. So did her foot. Now and then she checked her watch, which she'd set on the edge of the sink. She didn't want to be late to Dandy and Althea's but the water felt so good. . . .

Bahira woke with a splash when she slid underwater and struggled to sit up again. "Oh, that felt wonderful," she murmured to herself as she eyed her watch. "Yikes!" She surged up out of the tub, almost slipping and falling. Time had got away from her—again! What was the matter with her?

Hopping around, swathed in a towel, she

wiped the mirror clean of steam and bumbled through dressing. Twice she had to redo her makeup because she saw Hawk's face in the mirror, not her own. "That man is giving me indigestion," she muttered. "And a mouth with a leer if I can't get my lip gloss straight. And I'm talking to myself all the time." *Hic!* "Oh, no, not—" *Hic!*

Cursing to herself, holding her breath, and trying to wrap herself in a peach and cream pareau all at the same time didn't work. It was the last straw. Flustered and red-faced after the third attempt at draping her dress, her hands began to shake. When there was a knock at the door she almost screamed, she was so tense.

It had to be Melda, she thought, returning her blouse. Maybe her friend could help with the pareau. Still partially dressed, she threw open the door, holding her pareau in place with one hand.

"Melda, just the person—" She halted abruptly as her gaze traveled up Hawk Dyhart's long body. She blinked twice to make sure, because she had just seen him in her mirror. "I have to go out," she said lamely.

"You don't look ready," he said, propping himself against the doorframe.

"I'm not. I'm hurrying and . . ." She shrugged.

"Let me help."

He pushed away from the door and urged her back into her room. The smile slipped off her face as alarm dawned. Her hands tightened on her pareau, and she was irritated to see his eyes light with amusement.

"I don't see how you can help," she said, trying to maintain some dignity. "I have to be somewhere in ten minutes. Excuse me."

She returned to her mirror, twisting and turning the pareau, wrinkling it. "I don't like to be late," she went on, aware she was beginning to babble. "It's not polite." Why was he there? she wondered. He'd just shrunk her already small room to Lilliputian size. She'd have to finish dressing in the bathroom.

She stifled a gasp as he took hold of her pareau, turned her about, and swathed the fabric around her body so that one piece drifted over her shoulder. She could only stare up at him. How had he done it so fast? she wondered, staring up at him. It must be because he was so used to dressing the cords of women he had stacked in his personal wood box called an apartment! Damn him. She turned toward the mirror, unwillingly admiring the fluid lines of the soft cotton fabric.

"How many women do you dress every day?"

Not until she saw his laughing face in the mirror did she realize she'd spoken aloud. She wanted to sink right through the floorboards to the first floor. Her color changed from peachy cream to blotchy red. "Sorry," she mumbled.

He slipped his arms around her waist, pulling her back to him. "Actually, I don't dress many women, but I'd like to volunteer if you need a dresser." His gaze dropped to her mouth as she bit her lip. "And I'd like to do that for you too."

"What?" Her voice was a mere croak.

"Bite your lip." He kissed her ear. "Suck on it," he said more softly.

"Oh." She could barely swallow. "Cannibal." Her squeaky tone elicited a chuckle from him.

"You make me laugh, Bahira Massoud." He tightened his hold on her.

She shook her head. "I don't know what made me say that. I don't—" Her gaze fell on her alarm clock. "I've got to go or I'll miss the bus."

"Don't worry. I'll get you there."

"You will? Why? I mean, I'm joining friends at their house." She couldn't seem to sort out her jumbled thoughts. Hawk Dyhart made her crazy. But he looked beautiful. He had on an island cotton shirt in a deep brown hue with large golden flowers splashed across it. The colors were like his eyes, and made his skin appear a deeper bronze. His brown cotton dungarees were a shade lighter than his leather espadrilles. He looked capable and expensive. She would have to eat one meal a day for several weeks to be able to afford his clothes.

"You look handsome," she said, then groaned. Lord! Was she never going to stop putting her foot in it? As she fumbled for an explanation for her impertinence, she was taken aback by his blush. Speechless, she studied him, entranced by the sight of the sophisticated Hawk Dyhart being thrown off stride. Somehow it mitigated all that had happened between them to know that he could be as unsteady as she.

"Thank you," Hawk said huskily. Other women had complimented him, even been more flattering, their remarks purposefully provocative. Like water down a sluice, they had always washed over him, leaving no dent or lasting imprint. Bahira Massoud had just struck him in the chest with her words, and he was staggered at the blow and their power. "Shall we go?" he asked hoarsely.

"If you're sure you don't mind. Do you have a car?" Bahira asked as she preceded him out the door, then gave him her key so that he could lock it.

"No," he said. "Harry's driving us, then he's going to drop off a car—"

"Harry! Haven't you learned your lesson?" She laughed at his grimace, but then the laughter caught when he took her arm to lead her down the stairs. Even just that gentlemanly gesture set her heart pounding with joy.

"I don't intend to have any of his tea," Hawk said, tucking her arm in his as they crossed the courtyard.

Bahira chuckled. She was about to ask him why he'd come to her door when Harry drove up, screeching to a stop and spraying them with stones. "Harry, be careful," she exclaimed.

"Bahira, my girl," Harry said, "you should relax more. Look at how it's helped me. Hop in and we'll be on our way. You're my only passengers this trip." He beamed at them.

"We were last time, too, Harry," she said dampeningly.

Harry ignored that, closed the door after them, and shot down the narrow highway with whiplash force. "I'll have me best car at your door when you're ready to come home, Mr. Dyhart, sir," he said, grinning at them in the rearview mirror.

Bahira turned to Hawk, hesitant but curious. "Where are you going?" Flustered, she waved her hand at him. "I don't mean to be nosy. I just thought it wouldn't be necessary for you to come. . . . That is, Harry could've taken me . . . not that I'm not happy you're here. . . ." She subsided, telling herself to quit before she made it worse.

Hawk leaned toward her, his mouth mere centimeters from her ear. "I called Dandy's wife and told her I wanted to be your date tonight." He paused when her head whipped his way. "Angry with me?"

"Surprised." And delighted. Stunned. Jumping for joy.

"I know it might seem pushy to you." He had been trying to rationalize to himself why he'd done it. It was going to be impossible to explain it to her when he wasn't damn sure of most of his actions that day. If anyone on his staff had acted so nonsensically, he'd have sent him or her on a long, long vacation.

Bahira was intrigued . . . and pleased to see Hawk so ill at ease. "I don't mind," she said. "But I'll admit I'm curious."

"I wanted to be with you," he said simply. That didn't explain everything he'd done that day, but it was the underlying truth. To hell with anything else, he thought, and kissed her ear.

She turned her head, and their lips met lightly. She pulled back a fraction so she could see him, but she didn't speak.

"What are you thinking?" he asked anxiously. If truth be told, he didn't like his reactions to her. She excited him, but then she unnerved him because he couldn't tell what she was thinking or feeling. She had him dangling, dammit! He hated that sensation.

"I'm thinking that I like being with you," she confessed. She added silently that being with him could destroy her if she was foolish enough to fall in love with him. She took a deep breath. No, she wouldn't do that. Hadn't she had enough pain in her life? She could control her feelings for Hawk, keep everything in perspective. "I'm getting smarter about things like this," she said confidingly.

"About what?"

"I don't get as intense as I once did. Like you and me, for instance. It's just an evening, a moment in time. Why make a big deal of it? Right?"

"Right," Hawk said slowly. Wrenching disappointment, anger, and bitter amusement all crowded together in a rush of emotion through him.

"I think you'll like Althea," she added blithely.

Just an evening. Hawk thought. Hell! She

gut-punched him, knocking the breath out of him, then prattled on about liking her friend. Did she really see him as no more than a guest? Hurt was an acid that ate through his chest. "I'm sure I will like her," he said stiffly.

She looked at him inquiringly, but he refused to meet her eyes. They remained silent as the bus slowly climbed a hill, then stopped just below the crest in front of a house.

"Here we are," Harry boomed to his quiet passengers. "The car will be here when you come out." He frowned at the thoughtful pair who exited his bus, then smiled again when Hawk pushed a twenty into his hand. "I'm sure you'll have a foine time," he said, then drove away, the bus spitting stones and dust.

Dandy and Althea's house was small, but the lanai formed a wide U around it, overlooking the thick jungle growth that covered the narrow lot. At one point on the lanai there was a fine view of the sea.

Dandy rushed to meet them as they stepped onto the lanai. He kissed Bahira on the cheek and shook Hawk's hand. "Hi, Bahira. I'm glad you're here, Mr. Dyhart. We've got music and dancing."

"Your cousins?" Bahira asked. She was very conscious of the man behind her, his hand lightly touching her waist.

"Yep," Dandy said. "And they're hot tonight. Come and get something to drink and meet everyone."

They were whirled through the introductions

to Dandy and Althea's family and friends. Some Bahira had met before, others were new to her. She was strangely proud of the easy way Hawk handled the introductions and idle chatter.

"Here, Bahira," Dandy said, handing her a frothy pale yellow drink. "Fresh piña colada, no rum. I made it myself."

"Thank you, my favorite." She sipped the rich drink, glad of something to concentrate on besides Hawk Dyhart. A few of the women guests were eyeing him. When one winked at him, Bahira gasped and took too big a swallow. Instantly, she began to cough, then hiccup.

"Upset about something?" Hawk asked as he returned to her, a glass of the local beer in his hand. "Don't fight the hiccups, love. Relax, hold your breath, relax." He took her drink and set it and his beer down on a nearby table. "We'll dance. That should help." He pulled her into his arms, holding her close, his chin against her hair. As they swayed to the soft island music, he felt the now-familiar rush of blood through his veins.

He called her *love!* Bahira thought. She'd heard him. *Hic!* Oh, damn. Cuddling close to him, she tried not to hiccup into his shirt. She did. His chuckle made her smile, although she didn't look up at him. His body was so hard, so protective. When he'd put his arms around her, she'd felt as if she'd stepped into a new world. She fought the sensation of being cosseted, cushioned from life's slings and arrows. That wasn't for her. She lived in the real world.

Tonight was a dream, wonderful while it lasted but not a forever thing.

The evening whirled by. Bahira danced with other men; Hawk danced with Althea and some of the other women. Mostly, though, they danced with each other. When they weren't dancing, but simply standing and talking to people, they remained close, their bodies almost touching.

Bahira could feel his laughter.

Hawk could feel her breathing, could sense her smile before she did.

The dinner of broiled dolphin fish and green salad was a huge success. Wine, beer, and cocktails flowed freely, though Bahira noticed that Hawk nursed his drink. Every time she looked at him, she felt totally at peace, and was almost amused at how much she wanted him. What a relief it was to let go of her emotions, to admit he intrigued her as no person ever had, to say yes to the throbbing desire that both filled her with trepidation and fired her so very deeply.

Maybe they could have more, she thought daringly. For a moment hope sprang in her like a gusher. Then she tamped it down and brought reason into play. Hawk didn't want entanglements. He was rich, and she was sure he liked living in the fast lane and had a host of beautiful women to entertain him. This was an interlude for him, as it was for her.

She forced down the inner voice that wanted to argue, reminding herself that she liked her life. She relished the battle to struggle back up from the bottom. And she was getting there. Going back to the frothy existence she'd once lived didn't appeal to her in the slightest. She knew that would surprise her uncle and cousin. But though being spoiled and indulged was fine for a day or two, a lifetime of it could be stifling. How often had she been bored when she was younger? She certainly didn't have time for that now.

No, she mused, this interlude with Hawk would be wonderful—but fleeting. Their lifestyles were poles apart. Anything longer than a short liaison wouldn't work. After all, it would only be a sexual relationship, and such relationships were usually of short duration. Even if it were longer, even if he married her, would she ever be important to him? No. Better to keep it light, then say good-bye. She knew she'd miss him, but better that than to disappear into the fluffy, choking fabric of a shaky marriage. She loved him too much for that.

Love! The thought actually staggered her, and Hawk turned to her in concern.

"Easy there," he said, "What's wrong?" He took her drink from her and set it on the railing of the lanai, then peered closely at her. "Are you in pain? You've turned so white." He leaned over her. "Your foot?"

She smiled weakly and shook her head. "Maybe too much good food." What an agonizing revelation! *Hic!*

"Hiccups again?" He frowned. "Have you always had this problem? Maybe you should talk to your physician."

Hic! "I'll do that." What a mess, she thought. Bahira Massoud, you're a fool. Just what she needed, one more hurdle in a life of high jumps. She stared up at him, assessing him feature by feature. She could have this night, this one night . . . and she was going to take it, even if she had to seduce him. That decision made, her worries dropped off her like insubstantial cobwebs. She'd be his woman, and he'd be her man—one time, and one time only. She wasn't going to change her life; he'd never change his. Nor could she be his mistress. It would be too destructive to her inner self, and over a long term, it would be a slow suicide of her spirit. She couldn't do that to herself, or to him. Their relationship would sour until they hated each other. No! She didn't want that. She looked up at him.

"What are you thinking?" Hawk loved the glowing look in her eyes. Unless he was blind and didn't know women at all, he saw desire there, a want as great as his own. His heart pounded hard. "Tell me," he whispered.

"I was thinking about you . . . and about going to your place."

He touched her face, his hand trembling. "Are we going to my place, Bahira?" His heart felt as if it were doing back flips. She wanted to come home with him! Happiness roared through him like a flash flood. He could have shouted with joy, laughed out loud, bought the world a round of mai tais.

Her eyes avoided his. "Yes," she said hesitantly. "Unless you'd rather not."

Her husky voice stroked his senses like the
most erotic caress. "I'd rather." He moved so that
he blocked her from the others, then lifted her
hand to his mouth, turning it so he could press
his lips to her palm.

Bahira couldn't have moved if she'd been
prodded with a gun. "I . . . I'd rather too."

"Shall we inform our host and hostess that
we'll be leaving?" Excitement built in him like
lava behind rock until he thought he'd burst
into a million happy fragments. And all he'd
done was kiss her hand. Later, at his place, he
would kiss all of her, hipbone, anklebone, toe,
eyebrow, and everything in between. And if he
didn't start soon, he'd do it right there.

As though it had a mind of its own Bahira's
hand touched his face, stroked down his cheek.
He closed his eyes in pleasure, and she felt her
own body begin to tremble. "Dandy's over there,"
she said absently.

"What are you thinking?"

"I was wondering when you were going to kiss
my mouth."

Hawk felt as though he'd been paralyzed. He
couldn't have looked away from her if he'd tried,
and he didn't want to do that. "Let's find Dandy
and his wife," he said huskily.

She nodded, feeling energized, impatient, yet
serene too. It was wonderful. Not for a long time
had she felt such peace and certainty. Hawk's
eyes were hot, making her mouth go dry. When

he took her hand, she closed her fingers tight around his.

Hawk felt great. Sensations older than the pyramids flooded him. He wanted her, and she wanted him. It was enough. He wouldn't allow the voice inside him reminding him he'd want more to bother him. They'd settle that tomorrow. He already knew he didn't want to let her go. His long legs carried him halfway across the lanai before he stopped, realizing he was all but pulling her off her feet. "I guess I'm in a hurry."

His husky whisper was like a caress, his twisted smile was its own embrace. Bahira staggered against the railing. "Sorry. I guess the wine's hitting me."

"You didn't have any," he said softly, his mouth brushing her ear. "You had a piña colada without rum." His hand massaged her hip.

His touch melted her, sending scissors of heat through her. She turned to face Dandy, who had walked over to them and was gazing at her questioningly. "Hi. Good drink. Good party. Have to go." She smiled limply when her friend chuckled.

Althea joined them and stared assessingly at Hawk. "Did Dandy tell you that we love Bahira?"

Hawk nodded. "There's a lot of that going around," he murmured, his hand tightening on Bahira's hip.

"Honey." Dandy touched his wife's arm, then he looked back at Bahira, his gaze lighting on the the hand at her waist. "I'll see you tomorrow," he said, then looked straight at Hawk.

Hawk nodded as though words had been exchanged between Dandy and him. Then he gathered Bahira to his side and directed her toward the door. The pace was slow because there were many people to speak to, good-byes to make.

At last they were outside.

Bahira looked at the vehicle parked in front of the house, then put her hand over her mouth to smother a giggle.

Hawk had been staring down at her, but now he followed her gaze. "Good Lord, what's that?" When her laughter burst forth, he shook his head. "That can't be our transportation. I ordered a car."

"A hearse is a car of sorts," Bahira said, giggling.

"True." His irritation melted away as her laughter floated over him. He felt happy, protective . . . new. He put his arm around her waist, lightly, just touching. "Lady, your chariot awaits."

Bahira managed to keep her smile, but all of her felt seared, by his touch. Ambivalent feelings erupted in her. Happiness, sadness, joy, trepidation. She was at peace with herself and yet out of control. Over all these sensations was awe that this one man could affect her so.

"I wonder," she said, struggling for some stability, "if Harry has any other surprises for you while you're on the island." But she didn't want to talk about Harry. She wanted to leave with Hawk, go back to his place, and . . .

He touched her chin, lifting it so their eyes met. When he saw the desire that mirrored his,

his heart thundered in a new, wild cadence. "I want you, Bahira Massoud."

"That's good." She reeled with the torrid feelings that spilled around them. "But can you drive a hearse?" Unable to contain her delight, she laughed again. She wanted to shout at the moon that she'd found her man. No other man would mean so much. It was bittersweet to know that one day she might have another love, but none so great as this.

Her laughter warmed him, joined with him. "I guess I can manage."

"Good." She walked over to the sagging passenger door. Hawk reached around her to open it, his arm touching her waist. She looked up at him. "It's a crazy world. Right?"

"Right. But I would have preferred something other than a hearse." He closed her door, frowning at the poor tilt. There were no safety belts either. When he got in behind the wheel, he had to force the seat all the way back to accommodate his long legs, and the rusty metal screeched and complained.

The drive along the narrow winding roads didn't take long, but Bahira was quite sure she wouldn't forget the crackling intimacy, the oneness she felt even though they weren't touching, for all her days. Even when she was a very old lady, living with fading memories, this one would be sharp and clear. The old, rusty hearse with the cracked leather seats, and Hawk beside her. Beautiful.

He pulled into a space in front of the hotel

property, but in a secluded section. "We'll go down a more private path to my place," he said. "I don't want to meet anyone else. Do you?"

"No," she said softly. When he leaned over and kissed her cheek, passion blossomed inside her. She turned to him so that their lips met, and her mouth opened beneath his.

"Bahira." He sighed her name, then jerked back from her. "We need privacy."

She tried to laugh, but the sound died in her throat. Heat seemed to emanate from him, curling around her, roiling deep in her being. When he hooked an arm around her and directed her toward the path, she felt as though she were flying. Then she was flying as he swept her up in his arms.

"Are you in a hurry?" she asked, hooking her arm around his neck.

"Yes, but I want it to be slow, easy, and forever," he said gruffly. Hawk's mind was in turmoil. He'd wanted women before, but none as badly as he wanted Bahira Massoud. He needed them to come together at once, and always. He couldn't explain it any better than that.

"So do I." She hugged him. No more games tonight, she told herself. She had no intention of hiding, what she felt. She would open herself to him, at least for tonight.

They reached the Coral Cottage, and Hawk let her slide down his body while he reached for his key. To have her rub against him like that was more erotic than he could have dreamed. He gazed into her eyes and smiled ruefully, knowing she could feel his strong arousal. "You're too powerful, lady."

"I mean to be." Sexual excitement shot through her, firing her with a potent desire to take, and an even stronger need to give.

In moments they were inside with the closed door behind them.

"Drink?" he asked huskily.

She shook her head. "I don't need anything. How about you?"

"I need you." He smiled a crooked smile. "Will you let me do something I've been thinking about all evening?"

"What's that?" Her heartbeats were totally out of rhythm. Her entire body seemed to be melting, as if she were being remade, reborn in these precious moments with Hawk. She wondered how the new Bahira would look, but not much took her focus off Hawk.

"I want to twist you free of that pareau, sweetheart. You're like the one and only Christmas present I've ever wanted to open, to keep." He whispered against her neck, "May I?"

"Please." She could feel his passion like a live wire that wrapped around her and coupled with her own rising emotion, threatening to overpower them. She'd had only one lover, briefly, just before her uncle's company went bankrupt. She hadn't liked the sex, finding it uncomfortable both physically and mentally. Her feelings for the man had faded quickly after they broke up. Despite those unpleasant memories, though, she assumed making love with Hawk would be better because of the torrid feelings he engendered in her. This time her memories would be happy.

She touched him gently as they walked into the dim front room. Neither made a move to turn on a light. The moon lounging over the sea sent its silvery rays in to silhouette them, and that was enough. When he reached out his hand to her, she caught it, her breath choking her. He kissed her hand, then released it. His wonderful long fingers stroked gently over the hint of breast showing above the edge of the pareau. The material caught under her arms was pulled loose, ever so slowly. Hawk turned her, and again she felt his heat as it entered her. She twirled, her eyes drooping closed, her mind falling into a happy limbo. "I'll get dizzy," she said breathlessly, feeling the brush of warm air on her skin.

"Not to worry, sweet one, I'll catch you."

"Good." She raised her face to him, her eyes still closed, and relished his slow kisses across her cheeks and brow. Then she was turned again. She heard his sudden sharp inhalation. "What?"

"You have the most beautiful bottom I've ever seen, Bahira Massoud." His hands feathered over her, clenching and unclenching softly, telling her of his want.

He moved away, and she stayed still. But when she felt his mouth press against her buttocks, she arched, gasping. She'd never experienced such a wave of sensual sensation. He kissed, sucked, and bit ever so sweetly through her silky panties, until her body began to writhe. Then he flung away the pareau and whirled her around, not rising from the floor.

"Hawk!" The cry was pulled from her when he held her body close to his mouth, worrying the triangle of hair there, sending heat waves crashing through her, passion ascending like Venus from the sea.

"Bahira!" He stood and lifted her into his arms, whispering love words, all the wonderful things he wanted to do to her body, firing her even as he turned to flame. His quick strides took him across the room and up the curving flight of stairs.

Bahira didn't look away from him as they entered the spacious suite. Hawk was her only focus. When he placed her on the large, circular bed, she pulled him to her. "This is fun."

"You sound surprised, sweet one. Why?"

"I just never got around to expecting that," he said hazily as her mouth roved over his face. The slight rasp of his beard was an amazingly erotic stimulus. "I guess I just never expected you," she added, running her hands through his hair.

He laughed, then kissed her, hot, needful. "I like it when you ruffle my hair. May I do the same?"

She nodded languorously, then stiffened, her eyes opening wide. Shock raced through her as she realized what he intended doing. He was moving down her body, then blowing gently into the triangle of curls at the apex of her thighs, kissing her, loving her. Sweet, wonderful lightning zigzagged through her. When his tongue intruded in the most elemental way, her body arched, and a surprised gasp was pulled from her. "Hawk!"

He lifted his head, his eyes glazed. She was most wonderfully wet for him, and he hungered for her. "Sweet one, I'm loving you."

"Oh. It's wonderful. Hawk!" She nearly screamed when he began a rocking rhythm with his tongue, pushing into her womanhood, sending shock wave after shock wave through her. Slowly, her stiffened limbs melted, and she lifted her hips to him. "I want you," she said clearly. Her hands tugged at him.

He moved up quickly and claimed her mouth, his heart pounding out of rhythm. He hadn't expected his control to slip so wildly. He thrust his tongue into her mouth, too eager for her to be gentle as he demanded her response. He was hot, hungry, and needy as hell.

Her tongue was as wild and seeking as his. She didn't hold back. She rubbed her thighs over his legs and felt him shudder. His hard arousal stroked her midsection, and she cried out with delight. She stoked the fire in him as he stroked her, and with the ministrations came a passion unthought-of in her life.

Hawk had meant to bring her to ecstasy before joining her, but just touching her was nearly enough to undo him. The wonderful, deep sounds she made in her throat fired his passion into hot lava, and he had to fight to hold back. Her breasts were flattened against him. He let his hands slide under them so that he was caressing their undersides. Then he released one and reached down into her glorious wetness, stroking her to shuddering awareness.

"Hawk!"

Her breathy cry stimulated him even more, and he laved his tongue along her cheek to her ear, nipping there, tasting. He rolled her onto her stomach and, kissed his way down to her toes, then up again, nipping at her buttocks, his hands busy with her warm womanhood.

"I can't . . . can't," she said, gasping. "Hawk."

"I'm here, sweetheart. I love your body." He turned her over, swiping at the loose wisps of hair that clung to her face.

"Thank you. I like yours." She managed a weak smile. "I feel like a wet noodle."

"You sound surprised again."

She cupped his face. "It really isn't what I expected." She paused. "I suppose that's stupid."

"No, it's wonderful." Hawk understood that she was telling him her experience was neither wide nor good. He loved knowing that, happy that he would awaken her to the joys of sexual love . . . just as she'd awakened him. Her touch had brought new energy into his life, an awareness he hadn't even known was buried inside him. He reached up and combed his fingers through her hair, wanting to touch her, connect with her, every way he could.

He blanketed her with his body, and she loved it. Unconsciously, she began to writhe under him, loving the feel of his slick, strong body against her own, wanting the tight fire that enclosed them at once.

Now it was Hawk's turn to gasp. Her skin was silky smooth, but the slight friction she created sent his libido through the roof. Slowly, carefully, he began to join her. His aroused body nudged her sweet opening, and she surged against him. He grunted his satisfaction, his body tingling with a want that was like no other. He massaged her breasts, taking one into his mouth and suckling deeply. Her low cries of delight aroused him more, and he moved to the other, giving it the same warm attention.

Bahira squeezed her eyes shut, reveling in wave after wave of liquid heat. She wanted him. She hadn't expected to desire him so passionately. Hell, she hadn't even known she could feel such desire that she would be unable to hold back.

"Look at me, sweet one," he said in a rough, passion-filled voice. When her eyes opened, he smiled. "You're beautiful."

"So are you," she murmured, then gasped when his fingers teased the moist folds of her femininity. He was being so gentle. She dug her nails into his back, trying to urge him down on her.

He thrust his fingers into her wet smoothness, groaning his delight as he stroked her into greater heat. "Sweet one, you're so hot, you make me so hot."

"It's wonderful, isn't it?" He touched her again, and she cried out, a kaleidoscope of riotous colors swirling in her brain. Sensations branded her, fed her hunger with an ambrosia like no other. "Hawk!"

"I'm here, sweet thing." He kissed her gently as his fingers stroked the satiny folds, feeling her buck and writhe against him. "You're wet for me, angel." That relieved his shock at finding her so tight. He looked at her, noting her uncertainty. "I don't mind that you're not experienced."

"I'm not a virgin, either," she said, meaning to speak tartly, but her voice was too breathy. His low chuckle brought a reluctant smile from her. "But I never wanted another man.

Though he still caressed and kissed her, Hawk watched her closely. "And do you want me?"

She hesitated, suddenly fearful of the intimacy. Then the truth burst from her. "Yes, I want you. Right now."

"And I want you," he said huskily. His hand moved again. "You are so tight, sweet one."

"Can't help it." She gripped his satiny shaft, feeling it quiver at her touch. "I've never liked anything more." She stroked him, and heard him groan.

He grabbed her hand, pulling it away from him, ending the wild, sweet anguish that threatened to tear him apart. "Don't, Bahira, or it'll all be over before it's begun."

"We don't want it to be over, do we, Hawk?" Her eyes were heavy, her whole being languorous, yet she'd never felt such pulsing, exciting energy.

"Never," he whispered. The word was a covenant

he'd had no intention of giving, but once spoken, he felt no need to call it back. He embraced her more fully. "I won't let it end," he said, his mouth sliding down her body.

"Hawk?"

"Shh, love, I want to make it easier for you." And more joyous for him, he added silently. When his mouth reached the center of her femininity, his eagerness to taste her again had his heart thudding out of rhythm. He needed her! That was a shock, but a delightful one. As his tongue entered her in the most intimate way, his whole life changed his inner self beginning to make the wondrous commitment he never thought he'd have. Bahira! Sweet beautiful lady. His body seemed to rocket into the stratosphere as he delved deep into her being.

"Hawk!" Wild feelings tumbled through Bahira. She'd turned into a cascade, a river of emotions that she'd never known existed, that she'd never dreamed could be part of her. She clutched his shoulders, her fingers digging into him. She wanted him . . . needed him . . . The realization shook her, made her tremble.

He looked up. "You can't be cold, darling. I'm on fire." His mouth returned to her womanhood, and he caressed her sensuously.

"So am I," she murmured, her body arching when he nipped gently with his teeth. "I never knew."

"Good," he said. Maybe it was foolish to want to be the first to teach her of the wonders of love, but it mattered mightily to him.

Bahira was caught in a splendid vortex, and she let it whirl her higher and higher. Her body flexed and tautened, wanting him closer, needing the fiery ecstasy that he was showing her, the delight that had her wanting more.

Hawk felt the trembling of her limbs, of her inner self, as her climax began. His own body shook at the knowledge that she'd soon be embracing him deeply. He entered her at last, feeling that tight canal surge around him. Even though this wasn't her first time, he knew there could be discomfort. He surged against her and felt her instinctive withdrawal. Instantly, he pulled back.

"Hawk?" she said, bewildered at his sudden retreat. It had hurt for a moment, but she didn't want him to leave her. She wanted him, and hesitated only an instant before trying to bring him closer to her.

"Easy, darling," he said raspily, even though his body throbbed for completion. "I won't rush it. And it won't be painful for you." He gritted his teeth, for even though he felt the need to reassure her, he felt the more compelling need to bury himself deep inside her. "It will be wonderful," he managed to say.

And it would be. He was certain of that. Bahira had trashed all of his preconceived notions about relationships, involvements . . . love? Could this be love? Love was not a word he used, outside of his family. Yet how else could he explain this need to keep forever beside him a woman he'd known only a few days? How else could he explain his certain knowledge that once they made love, he'd be bound to her for all time?

"Sure of yourself, aren't you?" Bahira said. But even as she teased him, she, too, knew it would be wonderful. After her unfulfilling experiences with her first lover, she'd wondered if she was capable of sexual joy. No other man she'd met since then had attracted her enough to risk baring all in bed with him. No man except Hawk.

"I'm sure that I've never felt anything like this," he murmured in her ear.

She tightened her embrace, pleased that he'd said what she'd been thinking. "Awful, isn't it?"

"Yes."

She laughed even as her body clamored with need. "I'm not frigid." She wasn't aware she'd spoken aloud until Hawk reared back.

"Hell, no. You're beautiful and hot, love."

"Oh!" she exclaimed, and felt herself open to him. Hawk! He was the meaning she'd been searching for. For years her job had been paramount. Life had been a cycle of survival, and she'd been running fast on the wheel. Sex, love, had been put on the shelf, on the back burner of her mind. Not now! She'd been waiting for Hawk, for his touch. She hadn't missed anything by eschewing sex up until this moment, because now there was Hawk. She also knew that even if she married another—because she couldn't marry Hawk, they were from two different worlds—she'd never forget the wonder of being his. Just feeling him inside her excited her beyond measure.

Even as she thought that, he began a slow, sinuous rhythm. Air caught in her throat as he delved deeply . . .

"Ohhh . . ." she sighed.

"What is it, love?" Blood and desire pounded through him like an insistent island drum. He was tangled in a sensuous web that enwrapped him with emotion. Bahira!

"It's wonderful . . ." she whispered, "and warm. . . . Don't stop." Her world had turned over; she was flying. Hawk was her only anchor. And he was a shooting star.

"I won't stop," he promised. "I never want to stop. You're giving me everything, angel, and I want to give it back. It's so great." His body shuddered as hers enclosed him, spasmed around him, warmed him, cuddled him so hotly, he could hardly breathe.

Bahira writhed slowly, feeling him deep inside her, fitting snugly, taking her, giving to her. It wasn't supposed to be like this, she thought hazily. Not this torrid, wild wonder. Oh, Lord, she was on fire!

"Love, don't." He gasped for breath as her motions caused him to pulse with a need to spill his seed inside her. "I want it to be good for you."

"It is . . . it can never be better." Joy was a river flooding through. She held on to him as she sailed away from the real world, spinning into happiness.

When he started to move again in the age-old rhythm, he felt her hesitate, then join him. She lifted her hips to take more of him, his moan of need exciting her. Flames flared inside her as he withdrew and plunged deep again, his sweat-slick body abrading her like satin fire. She squeezed him tight, her muscles contracting around him, imprisoning him, and was awed by the power that coursed through her. He was her jailer, even as she trapped him. She wanted all from him even as she felt an almighty need to give everything to him.

Hawk tried to go slow, tried not to force on her the fierce cadence his body demanded. Wild as it was, he wanted and needed her climax more than his own.

Bahira was desperate with wanting. She wouldn't let him go slow. She knew she was safe with him. She desired him. Hurry, hurry, but don't ever stop. Never release her.

Hawk felt her passion as though it were alive. He'd reached out, and she'd taken him. And the wonder of it flooded him. The tumult shook him, shocked him. Never had he felt so torn apart, yet so together. She touched him everywhere; he wanted all of her. And he'd never let her go.

In the slow rush to heaven he held her tightly, and she carried him beyond the universe. They clung to each other and called out all the love names that only lovers know.

"Bahira! Sweetheart!"

"Hawk!"

Love tumbled them, catapulted them beyond the world, beyond the universe, helplessly into the lovers' ionosphere.

Five

The days passed euphorically. Incredibly. Neither Hawk nor Bahira could believe the ecstasy they generated. They wanted more, they wanted to give even more. The Coral Cottage became their haven, their castle of dreams that none could enter save them.

"Dandy and Althea think I've disappeared," Bahira said one day as she and Hawk lounged on his second-floor lanai. Their vision of the sea was unobscured, their privacy complete. "Some other employees have asked if I've decided to become a hermit."

"What do you say?" Hawk never tired of listening to her throaty voice.

"I fumble and stumble an answer, and tell them I'm busy."

He sighed and kissed her breast, nuzzling her nipple with his lips. "My staff thinks I've lost my mind. I'm sure the rest of my business associates agree with them." He kissed her again. "You have beautiful skin, darling." He laved the valley between her breasts with his tongue, then blew softly against the velvetly skin.

"Thank you," she said distractedly. At his mention of business, her mind flew from Barbados to Chicago and the time when he would leave.

She'd withdrawn from him again, Hawk thought with concern. "Tell me, Bahira," he said softly, leaning back from her. She was clad only in her bikini bottoms, and she made his blood boil, yet she also gave him a new serenity. He felt a deep concern for her, too, and wanted to make all her fears and troubles his own. Especially the one riding roughshod over her at that moment.

She looked at him, inhaling shakily. "It's an old story, and probably not worth the telling," she said slowly. And she never had told it to anyone.

"It means something to you, so it's important to me." He kissed her lips. "Tell me."

It had been locked inside her so long, Bahira wasn't sure she could. But when she saw his worry, she had a need to reassure him. "It's a tale like so many in the eighties and nineties. Illegal arbitraging. We, my uncle, cousin, and I, had a company, Massoud, Inc., basically run by my uncle. It was a small investment firm, but it supported us, and the investors, very well. We were 'comfortable,' as they say. We weren't 'I own two yachts and an island' rich, but we had more than ample. I went to a private high school in Switzerland, toured Europe and Asia then returned to the U.S. for a bachelor's degree in biology. I was going on to get my master's when my uncle became involved with a group called Sapphire. They were introduced to him by his lawyer, a man named Wellington. It came out at the trial that my uncle's trusted legal adviser had colluded with Sapphire to invade Massoud, Inc., by leading them into bogus deals. Once they did that and the company began to sag in the middle, they had every intention of—"

"Stealing the liquid assets, buying the crippled company, then unloading it piecemeal on the market," Hawk said heavily, hugging her. His body shook with anger.

"I can see you know the type," she said, smiling faintly. She leaned against him, strangely happy and relieved that she'd told him. She'd been carrying the knowledge around for years, like a damnable millstone. "My uncle is a wonderful, giving man, and I think that's what hurt my cousin and me the most. When he discovered his lawyer's perfidy, this man who had been a friend for years, Uncle Mohammar seemed to wither before our eyes." She sighed. It was like therapy, opening up to Hawk. The weight from years of worry and too-hard work began to dissipate.

"Has your uncle been ill?" Hawk asked, silently damning Sapphire and all business thieves. He'd always thought them contemptible. Now that they'd hit at Bahira, he found himself wanting to annihilate them.

"At first," she answered. "He couldn't sleep, and wouldn't eat. He worried Karim and me because he tried to carry it all on his shoulders. We hate that, and have discussed it with him more than once. He'll concede he's been too obscure and tell us he'll try to be more open, but it's his nature to take all responsibility." She smiled shakily. "He was cleared of all culpability at the trial, and he's been fighting back ever since, trying to rebuild Massoud, Inc. No one thought he could do it. Even Karim and I were skeptical. But he's managing to protect his investors to an amazing degree, and last year's profits were almost eighty percent of what they were before Sapphire hit. Uncle Mohammar is a wonderful man, Hawk. You'd like him."

"How could I help it? I'm crazy about his niece." He swallowed her laugh when he kissed her, his hands urgently stroking her naked body. "And I want her all the time."

"She wants you," Bahira said, breathily. Could this fantasy be real? she wondered, not for the first time. They'd come together so quickly, like meteors crashing in the heavens. Could such incendiary feelings last? She turned in his arms. "Make love to me."

"Gladly," he said, then kissed her deeply.

Hour moved into hour, day into day. They were happy, and growing closer all the time.

Hawk felt he was constantly in a daze, but he didn't try to fight it. It was all so new. He was sure no one had ever experienced such joy as this. His cool, detached observation of the world had been changed to one that was filled with life and vibrant color. He'd never known such pleasure before, and it was all wrapped up in Bahira. He didn't even have to be sexually joined to her. All she had to do was smile, and he'd feel himself flying. He threw himself into this new world without fear or hesitation. All the successes he'd achieved in the business world, all the passionate relationships he'd had with other women, paled in comparison to what he shared with Bahira. And he knew part of the reason was because for the first time in his adult life, he'd allowed himself to lose control. He was eager to introduce Bahira to everyone he knew, and to tell the entire planet that he loved her.

Bahira continued to work, finding that her job had new dimensions, lusters, and facets. Colors were brighter, people were more interesting, the landscape had more brilliance both day and night.

Slowly, much of her clothing and many of her personal things moved to the Coral Cottage. Most nights she slept there, when she slept. She tried to be discreet, but she really didn't care if anyone knew. All of her life was in Hawk. One day she'd have only memories, and she had to build them now.

The days passed too rapidly, and the nights whizzed by. All her wishing didn't stop the passage of time, but neither did time diminish the wonder she felt with Hawk. She was giddy with it, caught up in a splendor she'd never known. Even when she worked and spoke to others, Hawk was in the front of her mind, first in line.

One afternoon, nearly two weeks after they became lovers and more than a week since she'd told him about her uncle, Bahira was struggling to concentrate on a new guest and not on the familiar image of Hawk in her mind. "Yes," she told the woman, "that will be no trouble at all. I'll just get a bellman for you. . . ."

She looked up to signal for a bellman, and her mouth dropped open. Just past the new guest's shoulder, Hawk grinned at her. For a moment she went blank as his hot gaze pierced her. Instantly, she wanted him, and she saw the same desire in his eyes. With effort she recalled herself to her duties.

"Ah . . . pardon me, ma'am," she said, refocusing on the guest. "Would you repeat that?" She tried to glare at Hawk but he only smiled lazily back.

"You said you'd get a bellman," the woman said, sounding out her words as though she were speaking to someone who barely understood English.

"Right," Bahira said. She shot a killing glance at Hawk. He winked at her. When she'd managed to connect the puzzled woman with a bellman, she rounded on Hawk. "Why are you here? That woman probably thought I was mentally deficient because you distracted me."

"I'm a guest," he said easily. "I have every right to come to the lobby and ogle the help. Kiss me."

"No!" she said sharply, then glanced around to see if anyone was paying attention to them.

"Lecher," she added softly, but she made it sound like a love word, not an insult.

Hawk looked thoughtful. "I think you're right. You're on my mind all the time. I think about taking you to bed and—"

"Don't talk like that," she pleaded as her imagination took over. "Get out of here."

"I pay my bills," he said indignantly. "You can't throw me out of here for what I'm thinking."

"It's illegal," she whispered.

"It's wonderful," he whispered back, leaning close. "I want you right now, naked and—"

"No!" This time heads turned. She blushed and tried to smile. "See what you're doing," she said through her teeth.

"Pardon me, Miss Bahira Massoud, but guests have rights too. You can't toss me out of here just because I want to kiss you all over—"

"For heaven's sake!"

LeRoy, her replacement for the evening shift, slipped behind the desk, frowning at her. "What's wrong, Bahira?" he asked. "You really shouldn't shout that way. Think of the guests."

"Right." She let out a slow breath and reached down for her purse, trying to hide her blush. "See you tomorrow."

"All right," LeRoy said, then added doubtfully, "Hope you feel better."

When she felt Hawk's arm go around her, Bahira sidestepped away from him, and strode swiftly toward the exit that would take her to the path to the staff quarters. As she passed through the door, he took hold of her arm and turned her to face him.

"Someone will see," she said, half-laughing, half-admonishing. "I can't lose this job."

"No one's looking." He gazed down at her, his free hand rising to caress her cheek. "Besides, you should keep your options open. A better job might be coming your way."

Without much difficulty, he coaxed her down the path to the Coral Cottage. She was so incredibly wonderful, and he had no intention of leaving her behind when he left Barbados. He couldn't. And he would use every persuasive argument he had to make her see that they shouldn't be parted. That was the most important thing in his life. Business demanded his presence in Chicago and the West Coast, but he couldn't leave Bahira. He had a deep-seated fear that he shouldn't, and was damned if he would, even if he had to move his main office to Barbados until he convinced her.

"Are you angry with me?" he asked. He stopped on the path and kissed her, lingeringly, compellingly.

"Furious," she mumbled, her eyes drooping closed. Her arms encircled his waist, and the feel of his bare skin underneath the string shirt was an intolerable stimulus. She wanted him. She always wanted him! "Outraged, annoyed, and chagrined," she added. "I may strike you." Sure, she thought with amusement. After that kiss she could barely stand up.

"Please do. Every time you touch me, you

excite the hell out of me." His mouth covered hers again, and only the far-off laughter and chatter of people kept him from taking her right on the path. Damn! he thought. It was only afternoon, and he could barely contain his ardor. And they'd made love before she'd gone on her shift, twice. "You're killing me, love," he told her happily.

"Don't interrupt when I'm losing my temper," she said, kissing him again.

"Sorry." The voices came closer, and he lifted his mouth from hers reluctantly. "We've got to get back to the cottage," he said, and inhaled a deep, shuddering breath. "I need you."

She smiled, feeling the same urgency. "I should go to my place, though. Remember when I said I want to get my dress for this evening and make the call to my uncle . . . ?"

"Do it later." Hawk knew he was pressing her, but he'd never wanted anyone so much. He shook his head and moved back from her a step. "I'm being manipulative. I hate anyone doing that to me, and yet I'm going it to you."

She laughed. "It's dreadful, isn't it? I find myself doing it with you too. You'll be doing some paperwork, and I want to tell you to stop, to pay attention to me. And you pay too much attention to me already." He smiled that crooked smile she loved so much. The heat in those golden eyes had risen to volcano temperature. "When you look at me that way, I know I'm on your mind."

"You're always on my mind. Sometimes I feel you're inside of me, even when we're not even near each other." He shrugged, embarrassment touching his smile. "Nuts. Right?"

"If it is, I should be committed." She sighed. "Let's go to the Coral Cottage. I'll pick up my dress later and make the call then."

Hawk grinned and pulled her close for a quick kiss. "Call from the cottage."

She turned, her arm around his waist, as his was around hers. "Can't do that. It's against hotel policy."

Slightly irritated, Hawk frowned at her. "Not if the guest gives you permission."

She shook her head. "I can't do it. I'll call from my place." She didn't explain that she couldn't take it from him, a phone call, a gift, anything that smacked of "keeping." Maybe she was being "kept" in some measure, she thought honestly. Hawk was sure bent on feeding her well, taking her to all the best places on the island. But there were limits beyond which she couldn't go. Her sense of self demanded that.

"What shall we do tonight?" he asked as they approached the Coral Cottage. Touched by sea breezes, the thick wall of palms that shielded them from the other guests provided a soft crackling harmony. Not for the first time Hawk blessed the privacy.

"Why don't we have a picnic, or go for a walk?"

He grinned down at her as he held the door for her. "Trying to save my money again? You're a very frugal woman." Pain flashed across her face, quickly hidden by a smile. He closed the door and leaned against it, then pulled her to him, fitting her back to his chest. "You're thinking about your uncle again," he whispered in her hair.

"Yes." She couldn't clear the huskiness from her voice.

"And it hurts you when I talk about how frugal you are because you had to be after the business started to fold."

"Yes." Tears clogged her throat, not just from pain, but from the poignant sweetness of knowing Hawk could empathize with her, could see inside her. How could he know her so well, so quickly?

He brushed a strand of her hair back and kissed her cheek. "You struggled with the loss of a business. It was a personal as well as fiscal blow. And you had to fight upward to get even again. Be proud of that, pretty lady. I'm proud as hell of you."

His heart thudded against his breastbone when she remained silent. It hurt to think she might not believe what he was saying. "I can help you," he blurted out, tightening his hold on her when she stiffened. "Please understand, darling."

"I don't want that." She turned slowly in his arms and looked up at him, one hand stroking his smooth-shaven jaw. "As you say, I'm making it. I'll continue to do that. And I suppose I shouldn't be bothered by it anymore. It's happened to so many." She took a deep breath, her eyes searching his. "And to tell the truth, I'm better than I was since meeting you, Hawk Dyhart. You give me strength." The admission shook her. It was as though she'd given over something of herself. For a moment she wondered at her wisdom. Then she smothered her worries and hugged him. "What's done is done. No big deal."

He stroked her hair, knowing her clipped words hid a wealth of emotions. "You're a brave lady, Bahira Massoud."

She raised her head and smiled. "You're a nice person, Hawk Dyhart. Compassion and empathy are wonderful traits." She grinned. "So manly too." As she gazed at him, she realized she truly had put much of her pain behind her. Touching the face of the man she loved, she felt a warmth, a wondrous comforting heat that hadn't been in her life for several years. And Hawk was giving it to her.

Hawk wanted to tell her how he could—and would—help her, and not just with cash. But he sensed she wasn't yet ready to discuss such life-changing propositions as a partnership, both personal and professional. Bahira was a passionate, friendly, laughing person. She was also proud, and she had been hurt. And he had made a promise to wait. . . .

"I should go back and make my call," she said halfheartedly.

"And so you shall. But I thought we'd talk first." He bent down and nibbled on her ear.

"Talk?" She turned her face so that their lips met. At once the fire flared between them. She could feel the torrid wanting tear through her veins, could feel his heartbeat accelerating under her hands.

"Well, not all talk," he admitted. Her breathy laugh made his skin goose bump, and he was amazed once again at the power she had over him, the force she could engender in him . . . and with such speed. Momentarily uneasy, he fought for control, even while an inner self reveled in his surrender to her. He would willingly give up everything he had to be with her.

His mouth slid down her neck. "What would you think," he murmured, "about taking a job in Chicago? No, don't pull back. No tricks or gimmicks in this. I just want you where I can see you all the time, and I do have a large organization where you'd be considered a valuable asset."

Her body stiffened, and he knew he wasn't saying it well. All the smooth sophistication he could apply to his business propositions had deserted him. What he'd just said could be misconstrued as a sexual deal. He didn't want her thinking that. She was too important to him.

"Listen to me, Bahira," he said gazing intently at her. "No strings on this, no coercion, nothing that smacks of sexual blackmail. Straightforward all the way. I just want time to get to know you better." He shook her gently. "Things have happened lightning fast between us. We need time to sort it all out, to learn about each other. Don't you think we have something wonderful, something worth pursuing?"

"Yes," she whispered. And she would follow him to the ends of the earth, if . . . "But my job is as important to me as yours is to you. I need it and I like it."

"True." He nodded, quickly readjusting his thinking. "All right. Fair enough. We'll discuss it. If you can't make the change, then maybe it's up to me. I'll make an effort to move my headquarters down here temporarily." He grinned at her round-eyed surprise and kissed the corner of her mouth.

Agog, she stared at him. "All the way from Chicago? You wouldn't."

He nodded. "I would. And I'm prepared to prove it."

"But your base is in Chicago. You've told me that. It's central to your operation." Exhilaration rose in her. He wanted her so much, he was willing to do this for her? Resistance to him was ebbing fast. "Hawk," she breathed.

He kissed her, feeling his heart swell at the melting look in her eyes. "Yes, my base is in Chicago. But you're here and you are very important to me. I need to be near you." A sudden hurt sharpened within him. "Don't you feel the same?"

"Oh, yes." Her smile wobbled. "I didn't know how we'd resolve the distance factor." Hope spurted through her that her future could be with Hawk.

"There won't be a distance between us, sweet lady." He felt dizzy as the reality of what they were saying tumbled through him. They were deciding their future. "So? It's decided? We'll be together?"

Bahira nodded, not able to form a word. She reached up and brought his face down to hers, pressing her mouth to his as tears trickled from her eyes.

Hawk pulled back a fraction. "Crying?"

"Don't look like that." She hiccuped, though she tried to smile. "I'm just happy, happier than I've ever been. Nobody ever gets the fairy tale. But you just gave it to me. Oh, Hawk." She tried to stop the hiccups, but couldn't. *Hic!*

Laughter rumbled out of him, yet beneath the amusement he was deeply touched. He'd never thought that he would feel this way. But having her so happy when he was so happy at their decision, to be together, was the most intoxicating sensation. Happiness such as theirs had to be rare. "Hiccuping," he said, still chuckling. "How romantic." He roared when she glared at him. "I can just see us making love down through the years. Me, panting. You, hiccuping. Wow. That's the stuff dreams are made of, sweetie." He didn't try to duck when she cuffed him. Instead, he bent down and picked her up, throwing her over his shoulder, and hurried up the stairs.

"Monster. Put me down!" Bahira ordered even as she began laughing. Was life supposed to be this good? When he lowered her on the bed, she rolled onto her back and looked up at him. "You should be ashamed of yourself, laughing at my handicap."

He leaned over her, his mouth inches from hers. "Handicap? Those hiccups are the most erotic stimulus I've ever had, Bahira, my love.

When you've done that during our lovemaking, your body clenches so tightly on mine, I feel like I'll explode."

His words loosed such a torrid rush in her, the hiccups worsened even as her body burned and flushed with sexy embarrassment. "Oh . . . Lord . . ."

Caught between passion and laughter, Hawk began loving her, his mouth roving her body as the hiccups made it quiver beneath him. "Darling, I hope you never stop this wonderful little quirk."

"Beast," she said, between hiccups, trying not to laugh. She was totally amused and wholly aroused. At ease and yet tense with desire, she clasped him to her. "I . . . think . . . I'm allergic . . . to you." *Hic!*

"Never." He kissed her lingeringly, her face, her breasts, her stomach. Her spasms of hiccuping ceased, gasps of excitement talking their place as she arched with each caress. He smiled as he nibbled at her thigh. He'd cured her hiccups!

Tenderness filled him as he felt her arms lift and encircle his shoulders. He wanted her so much. And he wanted those wonderful, sexy rockets going off inside him, as they always did when he kissed her intimately. Losing himself in his passion he pushed his mouth through the soft triangle of hair and blew gently. His heart pounded out of rhythm when he felt her wetness. Sighing he pressed himself against her, stroking her with his tongue, treasuring her, aching to bring her to fulfillment over and over again.

"Hawk! I can't . . . I'm . . ." Her words faded away as the fiery chariot took hold of her and lifted her to the sky.

"I'm with you," Hawk said, his words slurred, his eyes slumberous as he slid up and into her body. "Darling Bahira. My own."

"Hawk, I love you."

"Me too."

As the whirlwind captured them, words were torn away. Only their gasps and sighs escaped them as the wonder took them upward and outward, climbing, building, until the comet ride burst around them in a million stars. They clung to each other, needing nothing else.

And after they slept.

When Bahira woke, she oriented herself at once. She'd woken too many times in Hawk's arms not to know where she was. She leaned into him, smiling at his deep breathing. Low snores escaped his parted lips, but they seemed lacking in force.

"I wore you out," she whispered, laughing to herself. "I like doing that, my man." She tried to slip from his arms, but they tightened convulsively, as though subconsciously he fought their parting. She waited a few minutes and tried again, moving more slowly. This time he let her go.

After slipping into her clothes as quietly as possible, she penned him a note, telling him that she was going back to her place to call her uncle and cousin. She placed the paper on the night table, blew him a kiss, and left the Coral Cottage.

Sprinting across the compound, she waved to some of the guests and staff but didn't pause. She was eager to get her call behind her, grab her clothes, and return to Hawk.

After running up the two flights of stairs and into her apartment, she was a little breathless and had to pause before dialing the number in Los Angeles. Karim answered on the second ring.

"Hi. It's Bahira. How are you?"

"Cousin, it's good to hear from you."

"You don't sound that happy." Bahira laughed uneasily. "What is it, Karim? Uncle Mohammar is all right, isn't he?"

"Yes, yes, we're both fine. Health-wise, anyway."

"What does that mean?" Trepidation rippled through her. "I know something's wrong, Karim. Tell me."

"I don't like laying this on you, Bahira—"

"Karim!"

"All right. You know how we've been rebuilding the business, getting it back to where it was before Sapphire bankrupted us. Several weeks ago Father and I approached a major bank here in Los Angeles for a loan, hoping a little more influx of cash would put us over the top. Yesterday the loan officer called me and said the loan had been approved, and we could come in any time to sign the papers. I rushed into Father's office to tell him the good news, and he said . . ." Karim paused, as if he still didn't believe what had happened. "He said the loan was no longer necessary. He had nearly reached an agreement with another company for them to buy his share of private stock in Massoud, Inc. He was only waiting for my approval as a fellow shareholder."

"Did you give it?" Bahira asked anxiously.

"Yes." Karim sounded miserable. "What could I do? Father owns a majority of stock, and I certainly couldn't raise the cash to meet the offer he'd gotten, much less better it. And he seems so convinced it will be best for Massoud, Inc. He assured me that Dyhart Tool and Die is not a shark outfit and—Bahira! Why did you scream?"

"I didn't scream," she said dully. "I moaned." Dreadful fears roared around her head like leaves in a hurricane. "Is this company based in Chicago?"

"Yes. Hawk Dyhart is the owner. You may have heard of him. He testified at the Senate hear—"

"Yes, yes, I've heard of him." She swallowed hard, her mind racing. "Listen, Karim. I'm going to try to take some time off. If I can't, I'll quit. I'm coming home. We'll fight this."

"Bahira, we can't. Listen to me. We've talked to our lawyer—"

"Then I'll come home to be with you."

Her cousin's broken laugh caught at her heart. "I'd like that. So would Father. When will you come?"

"As soon as I pack a few things. There's a flight out of here to Miami in the early evening." She glanced at her watch. "In about an hour, actually. If I'm lucky, I can get a seat on it."

Six

Hawk opened his eyes, blinked, flailed one arm, then covered his eyes. "Bahira?" He yawned, then frowned. The stillness told him he was alone in the cottage. His gaze flew to his wrist-watch and he frowned. He'd been asleep for three hours. She should've woken him. She didn't have that much free time, and they needed to spend it together. What the hell was taking her so long at her place? Rolling to his stomach, he dialed her room. He let the phone ring twelve times, then hung up. At once he dialed the front desk, wondering if she'd had to go back on duty. "Bahira Massoud, please," he said when the clerk answered.

"She isn't here, sir. May I help you?"

"Perhaps. Do you know where she is and how I can reach her?"

"Sorry, sir, I don't. Shall I page her for you?"

"No. I'll look myself first. Thanks."

Scowling with annoyance, he pulled on a pair of shorts, threw water on his face, and donned slip-ons. Where the hell was she? He checked the message machine, but failed to notice the slip of paper that had fallen to the floor, partially under the bed. He left his condo, jogging easily. She might be on the beach talking to Dandy, he thought, and headed in that direction. He was bothered, but not anxious. He missed her.

An hour later he was more than a little angry and concerned. Neither Dandy nor Althea had any idea where she was. He'd checked her place twice. It had been locked and silent both times. None of her friends on the same floor had a clue to her whereabouts, but they'd smiled and told him she'd be around somewhere.

When he'd exhausted every possibility and come up empty, he approached the manager of the hotel. Albert Payton shook his head and mentioned company rules.

"I'm sure it's not your policy to give personal information about your employees to guests," Hawk said testily. "This is different. If necessary, I can call the home office and work through them, if you'd prefer."

Payton studied him carefully, obviously assessing Hawk's determination and possible clout with his superiors. Albert Payton had worked hard to become a manager. When he looked at the implacable man facing him, he envisioned all of it slipping away. "I'll be just a moment, sir," he said. He walked into another office and returned with a file. He flipped through the pages, then nodded. Ah, yes. My assistant mentioned this earlier. It seems there was a family problem. Miss Massoud took the evening flight to the mainland, where she'll be joining her family in—"

"Los Angeles," Hawk said slowly, grinding his teeth. Dammit! Was someone ill? Or had he somehow misjudged the timing on the business deal?

"Will there be anything else, sir?" Payton asked.

"No," Hawk said sharply, then spun on his heel and stalked from the office.

He returned to the Coral Cottage and made a few calls, his sharp, incisive orders making more than one person wince. No one questioned his decisions, but not all his persuasiveness produced a flight out of Barbados until the following morning.

He had to coerce, plead, and all but threaten the conglomerate of wealthy Bajians who owned the only private jet available, in order to lease their plane. It took time. Finally, he made a deal and was able to gain use of the jet at an astronomical fee.

At three the next morning he was at the small field in back of the commercial airport, the lone passenger in the sleek machine. He hardly noticed the plushness of the interior, the comfortable wide seating, the huge television, the well-stocked bar. He'd be flying into Montreal, not Chicago. From there another private jet would fly him to Los Angeles. He'd given strict orders to his assistant that there were to be no long layovers. He had to get to Bahira and explain, before her hot temper destroyed everything between them.

Bahira's trip was long and tedious, broken by only one stop, ironically in Chicago. She shivered as she stepped into the terminal. Wasn't it hard enough trying to banish Hawk from her mind without being in his hometown?

Bleary-eyed, she hurried to the far-off gate where her connecting flight was waiting. She didn't look out any of the windows. She didn't want to see any part of Chicago, or think of Hawk. Had his takeover of Massoud, Inc., begun here? Damn his hide. She hated him . . . she loved him. She could kill him.

She huddled in her windowseat of the L.A. flight, staring blindly out at the clouds beneath her. She hadn't even said good-bye to Hawk. What did it matter? He'd betrayed her. She'd been tempted after she'd thrown some clothes in her suitcase to race back to the Coral Cottage, wake him, and haul him over the coals. Yet she'd been afraid that her love would betray her as badly as he had. Even though she knew he had used her, taken the information she'd given him about Massoud, Inc., to move in on them and buy her uncle's stock, thereby gaining control of the company, part of her wanted to forget that and let him love her, just one more time.

She despised herself for that weakness as much as she despised him for what he'd done.

She closed her eyes and tried to wipe all thoughts of him from her mind. Her eyes burned with fatigue and unshed tears.

"Would you like a refreshment, ma'am?" she heard an attendant ask.

She shook her head. A dying person didn't need refreshment.

Bahira stepped off the plane at L.A. International, and felt exhausted, disoriented, and still reeling with anger at how Hawk had killed her love for him. Love? she asked herself. Is that what that whirlwind was? No! It couldn't have been. But it didn't matter now. It was gone. Destroyed. She wouldn't think of him ever again.

She swiped her hand across her eyes, then straightened, hurrying to claim her baggage. Out of breath and perspiring, she finally made it out of the terminal and caught a cab. Since it was still business hours, she gave the address of Massoud, Inc. Fatigue rolled over her, and she leaned back and closed her eyes. Hawk was there in her brain, big as life. She couldn't drive him away, no matter how she tried. He was a liar, a cheat, a thief, and she couldn't get him out of her heart.

"Here, we are, lady." The driver turned around to look at her, and frowned. "You okay?"

Bahira snapped out of her doze, blinking. "A little tired." She glanced at the meter, then handed him some money. "Keep the change."

"That bag looks pretty heavy. I could carry it for you."

"Thanks, but I'm okay. I'll leave it with building security."

A few minutes later Bahira was sorry she hadn't accepted the driver's offer. The bag seemed to multiply ten pounds in weight at every step. Red-faced and blowing upward to dry the sweat on her face, she wrestled the bag through the automatic doors and headed for the security office.

Before she reached her destination, a uniformed security officer took the case. She told him her name and that she was going up to the offices of Massoud, Inc.

"Twenty-first floor," the guard said automatically as he wrote her name on a label. "We'll be sorry to lose the two Mr. Massouds," he went on, then attached the label to he suitcase.

In the act of turning away, Bahira spun back. "What?"

The guard looked up at her sharp tone and nodded slowly. "Yes. Massoud, Inc., is moving into a new skyscraper five blocks over. Rumors has it they've been bought out by a big conglomerate. But I bet they'll have great offices over there."

"Yeah, I'll bet," Bahira muttered, her hands clutching her purse. "Damn him."

"Pardon me, ma'am?"

"I'm just talking to myself. Thank you." She all but ran to the bank of elevators and punched the "up" button hard. In less than a minute an elevator was lifting her smoothly to the twenty-first floor.

As soon as she stepped out of the elevator, she could hear the scraping, squeaking sounds of furniture being moved. Her heart sank to her shoes. She inhaled deeply, then strode down the hall to see that the furniture was, indeed, being taking from the offices of Massoud, Inc.

"Excuse me," she said to the burly mover backing out of the door. She slipped around him, then stared bleakly at the all-but-empty outer office. Only the telephone was left, sitting in lonely splendor on the floor. No desk, no couch, chairs, or coffee table graced the waiting room.

Biting her lip to stifle a gasp, she walked slowly toward the private offices. "Uncle Mohammar?" Her voice was quavery, hesitant. She cleared her throat and spoke again. "Karim?"

"Yes? Who is it?" The voice was muffled behind the conference room door. The young man who appeared in the open doorway was of medium height with black hair, thick and straight. His slight frown lightened immediately.

"I don't believe it," he exclaimed. "You made it. Father! Father, come quickly." Karim crossed the room and clasped Bahira in his arms, swinging her around, laughing and almost crashing into the wall.

"What's going on? Why all the . . . Bahira? My child, is it you?" Uncle Mohammar stood in the doorway, staring in amazement.

Karim put Bahira down, and she ran to her uncle, noting that he looked more drawn and gaunt than before, and that there was a bluish tint to the skin around his eyes.

"My dear one, my dear one," he murmured, holding her tight. "You're here. I can't believe it."

"I thought you needed me, Uncle."

He pulled back, studying her, concern obvious in his expression. "You look tired. Has something happened, my child?"

She bit her lip. "I had to come. Karim told me that you sold your stock"—she saw the quick look her uncle gave his son—"and I was worried."

Mohammar shook his head. "All is well, Bahira. There is nothing to worry you. Everything will be fine. That I promise."

Though he smiled, he averted his eyes from hers, alarming her. "But, Uncle Mohammar, why are you moving? You've always loved this building."

"True." He looked around, spreading his arms wide. "This is no longer enough space for us. We're expanding." He patted her shoulder. "But we'll talk of that another time, child. You must tell me about your trip and what you've been doing."

He didn't want to discuss the takeover, she thought in anguish, how Hawk Dyhart had doubtlessly pressured him into selling his stock. Did Uncle Mohammar know about her and Hawk? Would Hawk have been so unfeeling as to tell her uncle exactly how he'd learned of Massoud, Inc.? Oh, no. Even Hawk wouldn't have been so cruel. But then why was Uncle Mohammar looking at her so speculatively?

"Bahira," he said, "you must to to the apartment and rest—"

"Why don't we all get something to eat first," she suggested, "then we can talk. I'm sure you'd like something, Uncle, and—"

"You go to the apartment, child. The housekeeper will feed you. We dare not leave until we've been settled in our new place. Karim, get your cousin a key." He turned back to Bahira and smiled. "Then this evening we'll dine *en-famille* and talk about everything."

"All right, Uncle," Bahira said slowly, then moved aside so that a mover could enter the conference room.

"Here, let me show you what should go next," Uncle Mohammar told the man courteously. "I'll see you this evening, child."

"Good-bye, Uncle." Bahira waited until her uncle entered the larger room, then she rounded on her cousin. "Why?"

Karim shook his head. "So much is going on, Bahira. I don't even know all the details." When her eyebrows raised, he spread his hands expressively. "It's true. Father assures me I'll know all on the day we sign the papers—"

"Papers for what?"

Again Karim shrugged. "I assumed he means for the new lease . . . and maybe with the new partners. Father's been very evasive."

Bahira nodded. Her uncle could be both evasive and stubborn when he chose. She moved toward the outer office. "But he's sold the business, hasn't he?"

Karim nodded. "As I said, I don't know all the gory details, because, as you know, my father can be very secretive. But he doesn't seem too upset about any of it." Karim shrugged. "He seems to believe this is the best thing that could happen to us."

Bahira thought of how persuasive Hawk could be, and bitterness flooded through her.

"Has he been cheated?"

"Not from all I could get out of him, but he's not been too open with me." Karim frowned. "He still says the Sapphire deal was all his fault. He thinks he should've been more on top of things, that they couldn't have scammed him if he'd been more alert—"

"But that's foolish. That was all investigated, and Uncle was cleared of any wrongdoing."

"I know that, but he feels he's culpable because he let them fool him." Karim shook his head. "As though he were the first person ever taken for a ride. My father's Moroccan pride will be his downfall one day." Karim put his arm around her as they approached the elevator. "Do you have luggage?"

"Downstairs."

"We'll be home early." He grinned at her, and touched her nose with one finger. "Because you're here. How did you manage to get away from your job? I thought you were indispensable."

"I am." Bahira smiled back at her beloved cousin, then she grimaced. "Of course, I might not have a job to go back to because of my impulsiveness. But I had to come."

Karim pressed the button for the elevator and kissed her cheek. "I'm glad you're here. Father needs you. So do I."

Hawk landed in Los Angeles feeling rested. There had been a king-size bed on the plane from Montreal, and he'd used it. He felt fresh and ready to do battle with Bahira Massoud. His assistant had booked him into the Beverly Hills Hotel, so he hailed a cab, threw his overnight bag into the backseat, and directed the driver there. He hadn't brought many clothes with him, but he knew his assistant had taken care of that as well. He didn't have time for anything but battling with Bahira. That would take all of his energy. As the cab left the airport, he leaned back and closed his eyes. He didn't fool himself that she wouldn't know about his involvement with the Massoud company. Once he'd factored all the information, he'd come to that unhappy conclusion. He'd bet his hat that's why she'd skipped out of Barbados and back to Los Angeles. And she'd be fuming. Dammit, why hadn't she said something? He could have explained. He would have preferred to tell her himself, but her uncle had asked him not to say anything until the transaction had been completed. He cursed himself for promising to keep mum. The minute he'd decided to go forward on the deal, he should've told her. Volatile woman that she was, she'd no doubt hit the roof when she found out, and arrived at all the wrong conclusions. His own guilt about saying nothing to her only exacerbated his temper. He pressed his fingers to his forehead, willing himself to relax.

He exhaled heavily and put Massoud, Inc., out of his mind. He wasn't able to do the same to Bahira. She lived in his being like a white light that couldn't be doused. Sighing, he opened up his briefcase. Work might be the panacea he needed.

•   •   •   •

Bahira was surprised and impressed with her uncle's apartment. She had never been there, knowing only that he had had to sell the mansion she had grown up in after the bankruptcy. She'd expected the apartment to be in a shabbier neighborhood, a less modern building. Not so. He and his son shared the entire third floor of a fine apartment building in a good neighborhood. She was more than a little relieved that her uncle and cousin had been living in such an elegant home.

She introduced herself to the housekeeper, unpacked, then soaked in a tub scented with wonderful Moroccan bath essence. Not even that comfort, however, blurred the churning memories of the man who wouldn't stay buried. Hawk! She squeezed her eyes shut. Hating him was a monumental task, and very wearing, but she'd do it. Damn him for making her love him. He should be weighted with stones and tossed into the Caribbean. And she wouldn't even try to save him.

Yawning, she leaned back, her eyes drooping closed. She gave up fighting the image of Hawk in her mind. He was always there, whether she was awake or sleeping.

When she woke sometime later, she knew she'd heard a noise. And the water was cool! How long had she been in the tub? She glanced at her watch on the tub surround. "Yikes!"

"Bahira? Are you never coming out of there?" Karim banged on the door, laughing. "Father and I will be in the living room." He chuckled.

"You fell asleep in the tub again. You've always done that."

"Go away, Cousin. Or I'll come out there and bite you." She smiled, when she heard him laugh louder, then shivered. She gave herself a quick wash and rose, reaching for a heated towel.

Hurrying, she dressed in a brown silk skirt and champagne-hued blouse, and for jewelry wore coral drop earrings and bracelets. Her shoes were brown kid that were years old, but still smart and very comfortable.

As she walked down the hall, she caught herself whistling a Moroccan lullaby her old amah had taught her. Regardless of the circumstances, it was wonderful to be home. If only Hawk . . .

Her cousin turned with a grin as she entered the living room, a glass of apple juice in each hand. "You look great, Bahira. You should look like a prune after one of those damned long baths." He stopped, tipping his head to one side, his glance puzzled and searching. "And there's something new. A different beauty about you, though you've always been lovely." He handed her a glass. "Are you in love, Cousin?"

Liquid sloshed over the side of the glass as she grasped it with a shaky hand, avoiding his gaze. She shook her head. Damn Karim, she thought. She should've known he'd spot anything. Although considering the strength of her feelings for Hawk, despite what he'd done, he might as well have tattooed his name on her forehead.

"Where's Uncle?" she asked, and glanced

around the room, more to hide herself than to find Mohammar.

"In his study on the phone. It's the third secretive call he's gotten today." Karim smiled wryly. "Maybe it's his tailor."

Bahira noted the bitter slash of humor. "Now, you know how he is. You're the one who told me he's been more insular since the Sapphire deal. No doubt he thinks he's protecting us from hurt by not talking about the business. Why don't you tell him how you feel, Karim? You know how much he loves you." She sighed. "I do wish he'd come straight out and talk about Massoud, Inc."

"What would you like to know, child?"

Neither Karim nor Bahira had heard him enter the living room. Mohammar smiled at their surprise as they whirled to face him.

Bahira put down her drink. "Everything, Uncle. I though Karim could tell me, but he seems as much in the dark as I am."

Mohammar turned to Karim. "I'm trying to change my ways, son. I know you should be privy to everything. I will make a better effort in the future."

Karim gave his characteristic shrug. "I know you want to, Father. But you still take it all on yourself and—" A buzzing sound interrupted him. "That's the elevator. Did you ring anyone up?"

Mohammar hesitated, then nodded, his smile swinging toward Bahira. "I hope you won't mind, dear. It's business."

Laughter burst from her. "Hasn't it always been?"

A reluctant smile crossed Karim's face. "I suppose you'll want to talk to him in your study. We'll remain here."

"No, we'll greet him together," Mohammar said, somewhat stiffly, and turned to face the archway.

The door chime sounded. They could hear the housekeeper cross the wide foyer. "Good evening, sir. Yes, just go through to the living room." There was a muffled response, then the sounds of someone approaching.

"Good evening," Hawk said as soon as he appeared in the doorway. A glass hit the oriental rug with a thud, and he turned and smiled at Bahira. "You've spilled your drink," he said softly.

The housekeeper swept around Hawk. "I heard that. Don't worry, miss. The rug's so thick, no glass would break on it. I'll have this cleaned up in a trice."

No one said a word. It was as though all four people were entranced by the cleanup of spilled apple juice. Silence stretched tautly between them. When Karim coughed, three pairs of eyes shifted to him as though he'd committed a social solecism.

At last the housekeeper left.

Mohammar cleared his throat. "I think you know everyone, Hawk—"

"How dare you come here?" Bahira blurted out, her hands shaking. "After what you've done to my family—"

"Bahira!" Mohammar was shocked. "You've never spoken to a guest in such a manner, child. How—"

"Father," Karim interrupted, "I, too, am

shocked that you've allowed this man into our home without warning us. As a former officer in Massoud, Inc., I would like to know why he's here. As a member of this family, Bahira also has a right to know." Karim stared at Hawk, flinty-eyed.

"Oh, I already know why he's here," Bahira said. "He's here to make my life even more miserable."

Seven

Dinner was a series of sounds. Crystal touching china, an echoing ring; forks scraping plates, an abrasive squeak; cups hitting saucers, an annoying tinkle; and the worst, audible chewing and swallowing.

Mohammar had demanded that no more discourteous comments or remarks about Massoud, Inc., be made until after the meal. "You will not treat our guest this way," he had said to Bahira and Karim. "I want your word, both of you, that you'll say nothing until we're having our coffee."

Bahira had glared at Hawk. "Not that he can explain—"

"Bahira!"

She'd jerked her head in assent.

"Karim?"

He'd nodded curtly, then offered his arm to his cousin.

Finally, the coffee was poured. The house-keeper also set down a platter of fruit and cheese, but no one touched it.

Mohammar took a deep breath. "Karim, Bahira, Hawk Dyhart has purchased my shares of Massoud, Inc.—"

"We know that," Bahira said abruptly. "Uncle, I think—"

"Why don't you let him finish, Bahira?" Hawk said.

She stared at him, her fingers curling into fists. Though he'd spoken in a low, even voice, she could tell he was furious. Good, she thought. So was she. "Don't tell me what to do, you manipulating thief. I could sock you."

Both Karim and Mohammar gasped and stared at her in shock.

"Go ahead," Hawk said.

Mohammar sucked in a deep breath. Karim swore.

"Don't think I won't!" she said.

"I already know what your punch is like," he said easily. "You did try to blacken my eye once." He turned to her uncle, smiling. "I assume you didn't know about your niece's pugilistic talents."

"Hawk!" Bahira burst out. Her hand clenched around her crystal water glass.

"Going to throw it?"

"Please don't, Bahira," Karim said. "It belonged to our grandmother."

"Don't worry, Karim," she said through

clenched teeth. "I wouldn't throw this beautiful piece."

"She'll look for something less expensive and heavier," Hawk said.

"Now, see here—" Karim began, half-rising from his chair.

"He's right, Karim," Bahira said hurriedly. "I was looking for a rock." She shot Hawk a murderous look as she rested a placating hand on her cousin's arm. "Pay no attention to him, Karim. He's not a part of our lives."

"Think again, sweetheart," Hawk said softly.

Bahira's face flamed as her cousin looked at her questioningly. Her uncle, she was amazed to see, seemed to be hiding a smile. "Ignore him," she mumbled, her eyes on the napkin she was folding and refolding on her lap. "How did you get here?"

"The same way as you, I imagine," Hawk said pleasantly. "By plane. Although judging from your behavior this evening, I wouldn't be surprised if you got here via a broomstick."

Bahira's eyes widened, and she really was tempted to throw her water glass. Seeing his taunting smile, though, she subsided.

"And how did you find this apartment?" she continued stiltedly.

"Your uncle—"

"He was invited by me," Mohammar interjected.

Bahira turned to him. "But why, Uncle? Why would you possible want to do business with this—this—"

Before she could think of a suitable epithet, Hawk threw down his napkin and rose to his feet. "With your permission, sir, I'd like to speak to Bahira alone. It might be better that way."

"All right," Mohammar said. He gestured to his son to keep quiet, although his eyes, lighted with a curious gleam of pleasure, remained fixed on his red-faced niece. "You'll have privacy in my study."

"I have nothing to say. . . ."

Hawk moved swiftly around the table. Bahira was swept up out of her chair and tossed over his shoulder.

"Hey—"

"You are going to listen," he said grimly, then nodded to the other two and strode from the room.

Their voices faded down the hall. Karim looked at his father. "He loves her, doesn't he?"

Mohammar nodded, smiling. "More important to me, my son, is that she loves him so very much."

Bahira staggered when Hawk set her down after kicking the study door shut behind him. "Caveman. I—"

"You're going to hear me out," he interrupted her, his voice hard.

She stared at him. He looked as if he'd go up in smoke any second. Shrugging, she sat down in a chair near the desk, facing him. "All right. But then you can leave."

"Not unless you leave with me." He glared at her. "How dare you think all those damn things about me? Oh, I know you thought I was making a hostile run at Massoud, Inc. You don't have to hide it."

"You were," she said, lashing out.

"I wasn't," he shot back.

"Would you have gone after Massoud, Inc., if I hadn't told you it was making a comeback?"

He leaned toward her, his eyes glittering with dangerous anger. "I 'went after' Massoud, Inc., because I knew from what you'd told me that it was still rocky, that any arbitrageur, lawful or unlawful, could make a run at it. I did it because—" He broke off abruptly and pulled back.

She saw the blood rise in his cheeks, saw his jaw clench tightly, his eyebrows draw together as if he were in pain. "Why?" she asked quietly. "Tell me why." Hope, like an underground stream, was rising to the surface.

"Because," he said, his voice hoarse, "I love you . . . and I wanted a future for us. I didn't want you worried or as torn apart as you've been." Tears filled her eyes, and she quickly blinked them back. "I thought I'd tell you right away," he went on, "but your uncle wanted it kept secret." He shrugged. "Maybe he was afraid something would go wrong at the last moment. Like you, your uncle has been badly hurt, and like you, he can be overly cautious. But nothing went wrong, except . . ." He smiled wanly. "Except that you found out in the worst possible way."

She rose to her feet, tears beginning to leak from her eyes. "Do you know," she asked, a note of accusation in her voice, "what I've been through the past two days?"

He scowled at her angry tone. "You think it was a picnic for me?" He moved closer to stand toe to toe with her. "Finding out that the woman I wanted to marry thought I was a low-down thief!"

"You never said anything about marriage!" she shouted back.

"Really? Well, did you know I didn't have to mention it to you? Your uncle told me that it's still legal for Moroccans of certain backgrounds, especially mountain people like your family, to be married without the woman's permission or knowledge. For all you know, you could be married to me already!"

"Not bloody likely." She planted her fists on her hips. "I'm my own woman. I say when I marry, and whom."

"The hell you do. *I* say—"

The childishness of the conversation suddenly hit her, and she sank back into the chair laughing uproariously.

"Bahira?" Hawk said uncertainly. He urged her back up out of the chair and held her against him. "Honey?"

"We're arguing," she said between chuckles, "about something we both want. It's crazy." Amusement overwhelmed her again, and she buried her face in his shoulder as the laughter rolled out of her. After a moment she felt an answering rumble in his chest.

"Believe me, darling," he said, "I wouldn't have done anything to hurt your uncle or cousin."

"I know." She tightened her arms around him. "I wish you had told me, though. I was so insecure about us. It happened so fast." She sighed, reveling in the feeling of being held by him. "I was afraid to believe in you, believe in what we have. It was such a beautiful explosion in my life."

"Yes. It knocked me out how much I loved you and wanted you, but I knew it was real, that it was all I'd ever want. That's the primary reason I offered to buy your uncle's stock, to protect it, to take care of what's yours." He leaned back from her. "But it's a very good investment, and your uncle and cousin are quite capable. I want them in my business." He kissed her gently. "You look so beautiful. And I love you. Will you marry me?"

She nodded, then kissed him back.

"What are you thinking?" he asked. "You look dreamy-eyed."

"I was thinking of a friend of mine, Margo Griffin. Several years ago we all thought she'd died in an awful plane accident, but she hadn't. When she came back, she and her husband, Cas, found a love more precious than what they'd shared before. That's the way I feel, that I've come back . . . to you." She paused, thinking. "I think I'd like Margo to be my attendant when we marry."

Hawk kissed her deeply. "Yes, have her, or a hundred others, but let's marry soon."

"Yes. Soon." She reached up and stroked his face. "It seems so far away and silly now." She shook her head. "I wanted to hate you. But you wouldn't get out of my heart."

"And I never will." He laughed, the relief and joy of being with her suffusing him.

"Mmm. How did you manage to get here so fast? There wasn't another flight out of Barbados for twenty-four hours. You should have been a day behind me." Even as she spoke, she studied his wonderful, strong-planed face. She didn't quite believe he was with her, that she could touch him, hold him, keep him.

"I rented a corporate jet. For an outrageous amount of money, I might add." He smiled at her. "But I would've swum if I'd had to. I had to get to you. I knew what you'd be thinking, and I had to set you straight." When he saw a tear trail slowly down her cheek, he hugged her tightly. "Darling, don't."

"It tears me apart to know how easily we could have been parted forever." A sob broke from her even as she tried to smile. She gripped his upper arms. "What fools we mortals be . . . or something like that. Shakespeare might have been speaking about us."

He nodded. Wiping the tear away, he pressed his mouth to her cheek. "I love you, Bahira. Remember that down through the years."

She nodded. "How did you find me so quickly?"

He grinned. "That was easy, sweetheart. First I wheedled the information out of the hotel manager—"

"Wheedled?" she repeated skeptically.

"All right. I made a threat or two. Anyhow, I found out from him that you'd left abruptly because of a family emergency and were on your way to L.A. It didn't take much to figure out what the 'family emergency' was, so the first person I called when I reached town was your uncle. He seemed to know exactly what was going on and invited me to dinner." His grin became wolfish. "I think he's eager to marry you off, my sweet."

She lightly punched his arm. "Lout. But I do love you, and I want to be your wife, badly."

Hawk sucked in an uneven breath, his being exploding with passion at the hot look in her eyes. "What a place you pick to turn me on, lady. Locking your uncle's study door is high on my list of things to do right now."

"Not a bad idea." She tapped his nose. "But as for turning you on . . . I can do that anywhere, anytime."

"True." He loved her like this. Reckless, teasing, giddy. "You're wonderful."

It was a delicious, refined torture to be with him, Bahira thought. Her mind was filled with memories of how freely, how gladly, she gave herself to him. In the front of her brain, as if on a wide-screen TV, was the vision of the two of them making love, writhing together, wanting, needing— She had to stop thinking about it. It made her so hot. "Oh dear!"

He chuckled. "Remembering, darling?"

"It's awful." She tried to frown at him. It didn't work. She felt too dreamy, too full of hope. Her insides were gelatin, her resolve like softened butter. She looked toward the closed door, then up at him. "Uncle Mohammar knows everything?"

"Yes. We talked several times on the phone, discussing a variety of things—"

"Including traditional Moroccan marriages," she said dryly.

He threw back his head and laughed. "Yes. That was one of the more enjoyable ones. I must confess, I was tempted."

"Wretch." She smiled up at him. "I can't believe this, you know." She wrinkled her nose. "I suppose we should join my uncle and Karim and let them know we're not fighting anymore."

"Not yet. I've had to cross a sea and a continent to touch you again. I want more time."

She hugged him. "So do I."

The bright color in her cheeks and the lively emotion he saw in her eyes enhanced her beauty. To him she was everything. "You're lovely, my sweet."

"And you're beautiful, Hawk Dyhart," she murmured, then nibbled on his lower lip.

Heart thundering, he bent over her. "Stop it, woman, or I'll be locking that door and to hell with your family."

"My man," she said lovingly.

"How long were you intending on staying in Los Angeles?" he asked, trailing kisses down her neck.

"Why?" She pulled back, wondering at the abrupt change of subject.

He lifted one shoulder in a casual shrug. "I just wondered where you'd like it to take place."

"What?" But she knew. She just wanted to hear it.

"My, you do like to question everything, don't you?" He grinned.

"Tell me," she said huskily.

"All right. When do you want the wedding to take place, and where? I say right now. I'm impatient. And, as you know, I could rejoin your uncle, sign a contract, and we'd be wed according to Moroccan custom."

She chuckled. "Don't you dare. I want the whole nine yards, Dyhart."

He groaned. "Well, make it fast, will you?"

"I'll do my best."

"You'd better."

"Eager, are you?"

"Very. Aren't you?"

"Oh, yes. I most definitely am."

Eight

The California sun looked like the fruit the state was famous for—an orange—and was rayed with blue, coral, and pink against the unusual backdrop of a clear sky. No smog, no fog, no mist. The sun fired down like a hot spray. It was almost September, and it could have been blistering, but a breeze calmed the heat.

"What a beautiful day for a wedding," Bahira's friend Margo Griffin said. She patted her flat middle. "I'm glad I had the babies a week earlier than expected. I had a chance to regain some of my figure." She laughed happily.

Bahira smiled at her glowing friend. "You're as slim as a model, and you know it." She sighed. "You know when I was in Barbados with Hawk, I'd think about you and Cas and wish we could have what you do. I was sure it couldn't happen. Now it has. And I almost don't believe it." Her smile wobbled. "It seems like too much happiness for any one person to have. I want it to grow, yet stay the same." She sighed again. "I think it scares me."

"You don't fool me," Margo said. "It's not just the future you're worried about, sweetie. It's the present too. You worry that you love him too much. I know all about that."

Bahira nodded. "I know I do. I recall what it took to bring you and Cas back together again. It's just that sometimes . . ."

"Sometimes love seems bigger than life and twice as hard to handle."

"Yes. When Hawk holds me, it all seems simple. But when we're apart . . . The last two months have been so difficult at times, with him in Chicago so often, all wrapped up in his business. It's a side of him I've never seen before. When I joined him there a few weeks ago, to meet his family and friends and consult with an interior decorator about any changes I wanted made to his house, I felt like I was completely immersing myself in his life . . . and burning all of my bridges behind me."

Margo frowned. "But you do love him. I can see it in your eyes."

"Oh, yes. I'm fully committed to him. But I'm afraid of it sometimes. Are we good enough to hang on to it? Do we love the right way? . . ."

"Of course you do," Margo said bracingly. "He bought a company for you. I consider that very romantic and as solid as Gibraltar."

A reluctant laugh burst from Bahira, and she hugged her friend.

"Are you afraid of him?" Margo asked.

"Not in the way you mean. He's a very gentle man, but I'm frightened of the way he can—can . . . Oh, I don't know what I mean. But I feel strange, cut loose when he's with me and even more adrift when he isn't. I don't think I like that."

"I understand how that's frightening you, and I think you were right when you said you feel like you're immersing yourself in his life. But believe me, I've seen the two of you together, and he's just as immersed in you. That's a special love you share, and it took Cas and me a long time to find it for ourselves. Consider yourselves lucky that you're starting out on the right foot."

"You're wildly in love with your husband, and he's bonkers about you."

"Yes. But you know it wasn't always easy street."

"Yes."

"Now, enough of these fears. Today you'll be married in a civil ceremony. Maybe you'll even have a traditional mountain one too—"

"Which I don't even have to attend," Bahira said dryly.

Margo laughed. "No less valid. Now look at me." Margo took hold of Bahira's arms. "We either get Cas and the three of us fight our way out of here, or you marry the man you love."

"And you and Cas could fight your way out of

here just for the fun of it," Bahira said, not answering directly.

"Bahira?"

"All right, all right. I marry."

"The man . . ."

"The man," Bahira whispered.

". . . you love."

". . . I love."

"Good. Let me get your suit. I'll put it on for you."

"I can dress myself," Bahira said, but she really wasn't sure she could. She'd just admitted to her dearest friend that she loved Hawk. She'd been saying it to Hawk every moment they were together . . . but telling someone else was different. Like Caesar, she'd crossed her Rubicon. But why play games with herself? she asked silently. Even if life were going to be hell on wheels with him, she wanted him. She wanted to be his wife. She had loved him from the beginning, and she always would. He was all of love for her. Knowing that made her feel all-powerful . . . and very unsure of herself.

"If he gets sick of me," she told her friend, "I'm camping on your doorstep, Griffin."

Margo laughed. "Get a move on with those stockings, lady, or we'll be late for your wedding."

Dressing was a blur. Bahira welcomed the haze.

In short order they were out of the apartment and driving to city hall with Cas, Karim, and

Uncle Mohammar, in the limousine her uncle had hired for the occasion.

Hawk was waiting on the steps of the imposing building when they pulled up, several people around him. He strode to the car and pulled open the door before the engine was shut off. Leaning in, he stared at her. "Good," he said. "You're here. I worried you might get cold feet. That damned imagination of yours goes wild at times." He smiled crookedly. "I didn't want to go chasing after you again."

Margo laughed. "If she'd wanted to go, I'd have taken her."

Hawk grinned at the vivacious brunette. "I'll bet you would. You're as daring as she is." He turned back to Bahira. "You look beautiful, my love."

Bahira almost melted. *My love,* he'd called her. "It is a love match," she whispered.

"You never said a truer word, Bahira." Hawk reached into the car and all but lifted her to the pavement. "And I intend to prove it to you." He kissed the tip of her nose. "But I think you know it, anyway."

All those days since he'd chased her to California and they'd been together and exchanged love vows tumbled down on her like an avalanche, and she began to shake. Now, they would never be parted. In fact, that day they'd be joined! All the bolstering that she'd plastered on herself from the day she'd left Barbados began to crack. Her knees buckled.

"Don't fret, love." Hawk pressed his mouth to her forehead. "It'll be all right, you'll see."

"It's insane. It shouldn't work, but it will. We can do that." His flashing smile had her heart pounding. "Oh, Hawk."

"I'm committed to you," he said.

"And I am to you," she said shakily. "Maybe it was too fast, but it's right."

"Yes," he whispered, and kissed her.

Margo chuckled. "Enough, you two. We're attracting a crowd. Time to go."

Bahira turned away from him blindly, and almost cannoned into Karim.

"What is it, Cousin?" Karim took hold of her upper arms. "Look at me. Is something wrong?"

"I'm getting married. Let's hurry," Bahira said urgently. She was swamped in ambivalent emotions, whirled in a vortex of loving, wanting, and needing Hawk.

"What's wrong with her?" Karim glanced narrow-eyed at Hawk. "Maybe she doesn't want this."

Margo grabbed Karim's arm. "Maybe she wants it too much. That happens. Now, go along with my husband and let up on Bahira. She wants this, she just doesn't know how to handle what she feels. It'll come."

Hawk hadn't taken his eyes off Bahira as she hurried up the steps with her uncle. But at Margo's words, he turned to look at her. "Thanks," he said, his smile crooked. "What we have is so damned potent, neither of us is sure which way to leap."

Margo grinned. "Close your eyes and jump, hand in hand. Best way." She winked at him and started after Bahira.

Karim watched her, his arm firmly held by Cas Griffin. "She's harder to understand than Bahira," he muttered.

Cas chuckled. "All beautiful women are complex, right, Dyhart? It's wonderful. I know."

Hawk nodded and bounded up the steps, two at a time.

The building was teeming with people, but in a small office, a little corner of the world, a miracle took place. Bahira was awed at the potent force, the tangible explosion of rightness and completion.

The ceremony was simple and brief.

Bahira was sure she'd spent more time choosing a toothbrush than it took for her to get married. She looked at the wide plain band on her finger, then up at the man who'd given it to her. "It's done," she told him quietly. "And I don't subscribe to the old ways of divorcing, even if you do sneak around behind my back and marry me in a mountain ceremony later."

"Good. I agree."

Bahira saw how the judge was staring at them, and she smiled. "Judge Catman, we might be married in a mountain ritual next time. Good-bye." She turned away, then swung back to hook Hawk's arm. "Let's go. You're well and truly caught this time."

The judge swallowed a giggle behind a cough. Margo didn't even try to hide her amusement, though her husband nudged her, shushing her.

Karim and Mohammar watched Bahira open-mouthed.

"I think she loves him, Father," Karim said after a moment. "But I don't think she wants to."

"Yes," Mohammar said softly. "She is much like her mother. How she fought my brother and railed at him, telling him over and over again that she was no one's houri, that she was Western and would kneel to no man."

Karim looked puzzled. "Why are you laughing? Didn't that make my uncle angry?"

"Not at all. He told her he was more than eager to become her houri if she wished." Mohammar laughed again at his son's shocked expression. "They loved each other . . . just that way." He inclined his head toward Bahira and Hawk as they walked out of the office. "I'm content."

Karim studied his father. "Did you love my uncle's wife?"

Startled, Mohammar shook his head, but redness crept up his face. "Perhaps I envied my brother his great happiness."

Karim hugged him. "We should go."

Dinner was at the Chez Grecque, where the menu was French and the music Greek and rousing. Coquilles St. Jacques with Caesar salad, and crisp, hot small loaves of *pain de vienne* made one and all salivate. The sorbet was pineapple, and the dessert would be cake and pastries.

Hawk leaned close to Bahira. "You're hungry."

She nodded, her mouth full of bread, and

swallowed. "I wasn't last night, or this morning. Now, I'm famished." She dug into her salad, noticing her husband's eyes brimming with laughter. "You think I'm a foodaholic . . . or something."

"No, I think you're wonderful."

She put down her salad fork, not taking her eyes from his. "I'm afraid."

He edged his chair closer, his body all but shielding her from the others. "Why?"

"We jumped into this. Catapulted is a better description. I hardly even know your family, yet now I'm related to them." She smiled weakly. "I know next to nothing about your life in Chicago, I don't know if I should go back to work, or if—"

"We don't need your income," he interrupted, "but if you'd like to work, do so. I hope you'd choose to work at Dyhart's, but the choice is yours." He looked around, frowning. "I need to be alone with you. Would you mind leaving now?"

"I would," she said regretfully. "I saw that wedding cake, and I don't think I'll be able to resist it."

His shout of laughter turned heads their way, and everyone smiled approvingly. "Then I think we should cut it as soon as possible," he said, although for him, she was the only dessert he wanted. He missed their lovemaking, felt hollow without it. It was as though something vital had been removed from his system, and now he needed it back.

"You have a sweet tooth," he added, "along

with your good appetite. But you're slim as a reed." He shook his head. "How do you do that?"

She shrugged. "I exercise, and have since I was a teenager. And none of my family is heavy. You think I'll turn into a mountain, don't you?"

He laughed. "No, I don't, but I think I'd love you even if you did." Then he frowned. "Maybe not. Obesity could damage your health. I wouldn't like that. We'll both watch our weight and diet by eating good food." He glanced at the swirled tower of white icing. "And once in a while, like this special occasion, we'll reward ourselves."

"You've never had a weight problem." She smacked him gently on the chest. "Hard as rock." Touching him was a joy she'd always want. Hawk was a beautiful man. And he was all of her life.

"Please continue to put your hands on me, darling. I can assure you the rest of me will soon be hard as well."

Her gasp was between alarm and amusement. "Sexual innuendo? From you?"

He leaned over and nuzzled her neck. "You're my wife. I'm allowed a little double entendre. And I love playing the game with you." He kissed her ear. "Goes with the territory."

"Better cut the cake."

"Your voice has a squeak in it, and you're hungry again."

The sexy mirth in his eyes was almost her undoing. That come-hither look, as old as mankind, told her so much, and she wasn't proof against it.

"What are you thinking, beautiful wife?" Her wonderful features were so expressive, he thought, and her eyes burned over him like velvet fire. Her skin was satin, and he longed to rub himself against it, from head to toes.

"I burn everything I eat," she said inanely, frantically searching for the words, any words, to get her back on track. Hawk had great power over her. One look and she was a grease spot. There must be something in the Bill of Rights about that. Her breathing was getting downright spotty. "So . . . I . . . should . . . stay . . . slim. Maybe." She frowned, trying to remember what she'd just said. Her brain simply was not retaining. Weight. That was it. Tomorrow she was going back to her old menu of toast for breakfast, plain yogurt for lunch, and whatever was available for dinner. She was not going to turn into a mountain just because she was married.

"Time to cut the cake, Bahira." Hawk took hold of her arm and led her to the cake table. As he curled her fingers around the long silver knife, he locked his eyes with hers. They cut two slices together, then he watched her warily as she lifted the first slice, her eyes gleaming. He braced himself.

"Silly you," she whispered. "I wouldn't wipe this over your face." At his surprised look she laughed. "I know that's what you were expecting." She fed him the cake and let him feed her. Then they gazed into each other's eyes until someone coughed. Startled out of the romantic haze that had enveloped them, they resumed their seats.

The cutting and serving of the cake, as well as several toasts, took more time, and finally Hawk rose to his feet, tapping his spoon against his glass. "My wife and I are leaving. Please stay and enjoy yourselves."

"Where are you going?" Margo ask mischievously.

"Back to where it began," he answered, and grinned when Bahira looked at him sharply. "My wife and I extend an invitation to our guests to join us for Christmas this year in Chicago. We'll arrange the transportation, and you'll stay with us and meet my family."

Bahira opened her mouth and Hawk kissed her, then picked her up and strode from the restaurant, amid cheers and laughter.

"I should say something to Uncle Mohammar," she said limply, clinging to Hawk.

"He knows. I told him what I was going to do."

"Overbearing, aren't you?"

"Yes."

In a whirl of motion they were in the limousine, speeding to the airport.

"No luggage," Bahira said, inordinately happy. "Did you really mean we're returning to the Coral Cottage?"

He nodded, pressing the button to close the opaque window between them and the driver, and lifted her onto his lap. He rubbed his cheek against her hair. "I don't think you quite understand how I felt about you, Mrs. Dyhart, when we were first in Barbados. So we're going back and I'm going to make everything abundantly clear to you."

Bemused, Bahira could only nod. They were out of the limo and into a private jet faster than she could've imagined. "You are in a hurry," she said as she settled into a seat.

"Yes." He stared seriously at her. "I love you, wife. And I know you didn't know how much. Maybe one day I'll be able to talk about how fearful I was that evening when I couldn't find you."

He managed a smile, but the expression in his eyes revealed the pain. His simple declaration shook her as nothing ever had. "I guess I didn't know," she said. "I was a fool not to have trusted you, Hawk. My only excuse is that I really feared what we had couldn't be real." Tears slipped down her face.

"Karim told me you were tough," he said, leaning over and dabbing at the moisture on her cheeks. "You're a cream puff."

"Not so. I am tough." She touched his face, so close to hers, and saw the agony she'd felt mirrored there. "Well, maybe with you I'm a bit of a cupcake." *Hic!* "Oh, no, not on my wedding day." Gritting her teeth, she tried to force back the embarrassing manifestations of her uncertainty and frustration.

"Love, don't hold your breath like that," Hawk said, trying hard not to laugh.

"I . . . won't do . . . this . . . today." *Hic!*

"Darling," he crooned to her. "I warned you that one day we'd be making love and you wouldn't be able to stop doing that."

"We're—*hic!*—not making love." She rolled her eyes when his amusement increased.

"This is a private plane with a wonderful king-size bed back there and a lock on the door," he told her, blowing softly in her ear.

"Really?" *Hic!* "Damn."

Hawk roared with laughter, undid both seat belts, and whisked her up into his arms. "I'm putting a Do Not Disturb sign on the door."

"Don't you—*hic!*—dare." She let her head fall against his shoulder. "This is awful. What a honeymoon."

"It'll be wonderful."

"Awful." *Hic!* "Don't laugh."

"Not to worry, darling. You know I can stop those hiccups."

When he laid her down on the bed, she reached up and twined her arms around his neck. "I love you too."

He nodded. "I know, I've always known, from the first moment we kissed. But I love to hear you say it." He lay down next to her. "We need to understand this special gift we've been given, Bahira."

She nodded. "You mean love."

"Yes." He propped his arms on either side of her and gazed down at her. "I had no intention of meeting the love of my life when I went to Barbados. I was sure my life was full, but you changed that idea. I knew some interesting women—Oww!"

"Serves you right," she said huskily, then cupped his face with her hands and pulled him down to her. She kissed him warmly. "I knew you had other women. I just don't like it."

He nodded. "I know the feeling. When you told me your experience with men was limited, I could've jumped for joy. But I also knew that it wouldn't have mattered if you'd been involved in a torrid affair with another man. We didn't orchestrate it, love. Neither of us wanted this powerful chemistry we generate, but I think we would be nine kinds of fools to give it away, or let it go."

"Yes." She stroked his face. "When we were in Barbados, I'd braced myself for your going, figuring I'd live on memories after you left. It would've been tough." She tried to swallow the tears, but she could feel them leaking from her eyes and slipping off her face to wet the pillow. "It would've been hell."

"And impossible." Hawk kissed the trails of tears, emotion wrenching him at the thought of being separated from her. "I'm going to chain you to me. You might as well work for my company since you're going to be there every day anyway." He grinned. "Or I'll be your shadow behind the desk at the Grand Bajian."

She gave a watery chuckle, then hugged him to her. "I never expected it, you see," she whispered in his ear. "I thought that people made a decision about sharing their lives and that was it. Sometimes they'd live together, sometimes they'd marry. It would all be pragmatic, firmly and clearly done. I didn't know it would be a hurricane and I'd be blown away."

He nodded, his mouth coursing over her cheek, his heart hammering against his breastbone. "Pretty much what I thought too." He lifted his head. "Then along came a bombshell who popped me in the eye for rolling her in the sand."

She laughed. "I was awful to you."

"You were wonderful. I fell in love when you hit me." He leered at her. "Now I have to pay you back."

"Very punitive." She gasped when he slid his hand down her body and began a caressing motion at the junction of her thighs. When his fingers titillated the soft petals there and made them wet, she moaned. "Some lesson."

His eyes languorous, he stared at her. "I've just begun to show you how much you mean to me, Bahira Massoud Dyhart," he said, his voice blurred with passion as he quickly removed her suit.

"I see." Her body arched when he lifted her up and pressed his mouth to her middle, his hands stroking up and down the sides of her body. When he licked her breasts through her silken chemise, her breath caught in her throat. When his teeth closed gently over a nipple, she called out, desire making her body writhe.

He slid up her body, holding her. "Kiss me, darling."

The odd note of urgency and gentleness in his voice pulled a heartfelt sob from her. "Oh, yes." Holding the sides of his face, she pressed her mouth to his in a ravenous kiss. As her tongue dueled with his, she rubbed her breasts across his chest. It felt so wonderful to be with him again.

Passion coursed through them like wildfire, and they held each other tightly, awed at the power they generated.

At last Hawk tore his mouth from hers and stripped off his wedding suit as though it were rags to be discarded. Then he removed her underthings, his hands shaking. He cursed colorfully at his clumsiness as he wrestled with her garter belt. "I like you better in a pareau," he muttered. "Less fuss." He sent her a dark look. "Don't laugh."

"Why not? I'm having a marvelous time." When he lifted her to slide the panties down her legs, then pressed his mouth to the warm, wet center of her, she moaned. Her hands gripped his shoulders.

"So am I," he murmured, lifting his head. "A fabulous time." In quick, sweet thrusts he put his tongue into her. He felt her body begin to quake, tremors shaking through her, even as he trembled from head to foot. Slowly sliding up her, he gathered her to him. "Promise to keep me, Bahira mine."

"Hawk!"

"Promise."

Through the sexual haze, the thrumming

want, she caught the urgency in his voice, the wonderful words he'd spoken. He'd offered himself to her, wholly, completely, and asked her to keep him. "Oh, Hawk, I love you. I'd die without you." Steadying herself, she smiled at him. "Don't you know that?"

"Promise to keep me, then I'll know," he said softly.

"I vowed to do so earlier today. I do again," she said solemnly. "Forever."

"I vow the same."

"Hawk."

He knew what she wanted. Watching her, he entered her slowly, filling her, and her gasps echoed his own. The rhythm began, and they rushed to meet it, savoring every thrust and holding on to each other.

In an explosion of sensation, she took him even as he claimed her, and the pounding joy swept over them, marking them forever.

"My husband," Bahira said softly.

In sure, throbbing delight Hawk kissed her. "My wife." Then he reared back. "Oh, honey, I didn't take precautions with you."

"Neither did I." *Hic!* "Oh, dear, not again. Could it be? Flying high over the world, did we conceive, Mr. Dyhart?" *Hic!*

He pressed his face between her breasts. "Only if you want it. I'd love our child, but we can wait—"

"No, we can't. I'm thirty. I'd like a baby." She kissed him, delight making her glow. "One just like you." *Hic!*

Nine

Bahira yawned, then smiled. They were staring
at her again. "I'm not due until the end of the
week," she told her uncle, cousin, and husband.
"Could we get on with this? What were you
saying about the Japanese involvement—"

"You could come early," Karim said. He
glanced at Hawk. "She shouldn't be here." Then
he glared at Bahira. "You think because you've
learned a few things about this business that
you're indispensable. You didn't have to come
today." Worry made him speak harshly, and he
turned to Hawk again. "Why didn't you make her
stay home?"

Hawk shrugged. "She insisted."

"You're not firm enough with her," Karim
muttered.

"Karim is right, child," Mohammar said. "You
should be home, resting."

179

Bahira looked at her men and sighed. "All right, let's finish the Japanese thing, and I'll go." She smiled. "I like the business, and I think I'm getting better at it. Even after the baby comes, I'll keep my hand in."

"Ridiculous," muttered Karim, glancing at his father. Mohammar only shrugged.

Bahira almost laughed at the speedy way business was completed. When she rose, she smiled down the table at her husband. "Should we tell them we're expecting twins?"

"You just did," Hawk said, rolling his eyes when Karim and Mohammar turned to him with shocked expressions. "I'll take her home," he promised. "If you're worried, you can call her doctor and talk to her."

When they were in the elevator going down to the parking garage, Bahira put her head on her husband's shoulder. "I'm happy, Hawk. You did that."

"We did it together. I love you, wife."

"Kiss me, then take me to the hospital. I think I'm in labor," she said happily. "Just another wonderful moment in time in our lives."

"Bahira!" He looked panicked for an instant, then groaned as she smiled sunnily at him, "Dammit, Bahira I love you, but a few more of your 'precious moments in time' and I'll be a dead man."

She patted his cheek. "You'll be just fine."

"I know," he said as the elevator doors opened.

They both knew their moment in time was forever.

THE EDITOR'S CORNER

As summer draws to a close, the nights get colder, and what better way could there be to warm up than by reading these fabulous LOVESWEPTs we have in store for you next month.

Joan Elliott Pickart leads the list with THE DEVIL IN STONE, LOVESWEPT #492, a powerful story of a love that flourishes despite difficult circumstances. When Robert Stone charges into Winter Holt's craft shop, he's a warrior on the warpath, out to expose a con artist. But he quickly realizes Winter is as honest as the day is long, and as beautiful as the desert sunrise. He longs to kiss away the sadness in her eyes, but she's vowed never to give her heart to another man—especially one who runs his life by a schedule and believes that love can be planned. It takes a lot of thrilling persuasion before Robert can convince Winter that their very different lives can be bridged. This is a romance to be cherished.

Humorous and emotional, playful and poignant, HEART OF DIXIE, LOVESWEPT #493, is another winner from Tami Hoag. Who can resist Jake Gannon, with his well-muscled body and blue eyes a girl can drown in? Dixie La Fontaine sure tries as she tows his overheated car to Mare's Nest, South Carolina. A perfect man like him would want a perfect woman, and that certainly isn't Dixie. But Jake knows a special lady when he sees one, and he's in hot pursuit of her down-home charm and all-delicious curves. If only he can share the secret of why he came to her town in the first place . . . A little mystery, a touch of Southern magic, and a lot of white-hot passion—who could ask for anything more?

A handsome devil of a rancher will send you swooning in THE LADY AND THE COWBOY, LOVESWEPT #494, by Charlotte Hughes. Dillon McKenzie is rugged, rowdy, and none too pleased that Abel Pratt's will divided his ranch equally between Dillon and a lady preacher! He doesn't want any goody-two-shoes telling him what to do, even one whose skin is silk and whose eyes light up the dark places in his heart. Rachael Caitland is determined to make the best of things, but the rough-and-tumble cowboy makes her yearn to risk caring for a man who's all wrong for her. Once Dillon tastes Rachael's fire, he'll move heaven and earth to make her break her rules. Give yourself a treat, and don't miss this compelling romance.

In SCANDALOUS, LOVESWEPT #495, Patricia Burroughs creates an unforgettable couple in the delectably brazen Paisley Vandermeir and the very respectable but oh so sexy Christopher Quincy Maitland. Born to a family constantly in the scandal sheets, Paisley is determined to commit one indiscretion and retire from notoriety. But when she throws herself at Chris, who belongs to another, she's shocked to find him a willing partner. Chris has a wild streak that's subdued by a comfortable engagement, but the intoxicating Paisley tempts him to break free. To claim her for his own, he'll brave trouble and reap its sweet reward. An utterly delightful book that will leave you smiling and looking for the next Patricia Burroughs LOVESWEPT.

Olivia Rupprecht pulls out all the stops in her next book, BEHIND CLOSED DOORS, LOVESWEPT #496, a potent love story that throbs with long-denied desire. When widower Myles Wellington learns that his sister-in-law, Faith, is carrying his child, he insists that she move into his house. Because she's loved him for so long and has been so alone, Faith has secretly agreed to help her sister with the gift of a child to Myles. How can she live with the one man who's forbidden to her, yet how can she resist grabbing at the chance to be with the only man whose touch sets her soul on fire? Myles wants this child, but he soon discovers he wants Faith even more. Together they struggle to break free of the past and exult in a passionate union. . . . Another fiery romance from Olivia.

Suzanne Forster concludes the month with a tale of smoldering sensuality, PRIVATE DANCER, LOVESWEPT #497. Sam Nichols is a tornado of sexual virility, and Bev Brewster has plenty of reservations about joining forces with him to hunt a con man on a cruise ship. Still, the job must be done, and Bev is professional enough to keep her distance from the deliciously dangerous Sam. But close quarters and steamy nights spark an inferno of ecstasy. Before long Sam's set her aflame with tantalizing caresses and thrilling kisses. But his dark anguish shadows the fierce pleasure they share. Once the chase is over and the criminal caught, will Sam's secret pain drive them apart forever?

Do remember to look for our FANFARE novels next month—four provocative and memorable stories with vastly different settings and times. First is GENUINE LIES by bestselling author Nora Roberts, a dazzling novel of Hollywood glamour, seductive secrets, and truth that can kill. MIRACLE by bestselling LOVESWEPT author Deborah Smith is an unforgettable story of love and the collision of worlds, from a shanty in the Georgia hills to a television studio in L.A. With warm, humorous, passionate characters, MIR-ACLE weaves a spell in which love may be improbable but never impossible. Award-winning author Susan Johnson joins the FAN-FARE list with her steamiest historical romance yet, FORBIDDEN. And don't miss bestselling LOVESWEPT author Judy Gill's BAD BILLY CULVER, a fabulous tale of sexual awakening, scandal, lies, and a passion that can't be denied.

We want to wish the best of luck to Carolyn Nichols, Publisher of LOVESWEPT. After nine eminently successful years, Carolyn has decided to leave publishing to embark on a new venture to help create jobs for the homeless. Carolyn joined Bantam Books in the spring of 1982 to create a line of contemporary romances. LOVESWEPT was launched to instant acclaim in May of 1983, and is now beloved by millions of fans worldwide. Numerous authors, now well-known and well-loved by loyal readers, have Carolyn to thank for daring to break the time-honored rules of romance writing, and for helping to usher in a vital new era of women's fiction.

For all of us here at LOVESWEPT, working with Carolyn has been an ever-stimulating experience. She has brought to her job a vitality and creativity that has spread throughout the staff and, we hope, will remain in the years to come. Carolyn is a consummate editor, a selfless, passionate, and unpretentious humanitarian, a loving mother, and our dear, dear friend. Though we will miss her deeply, we applaud her decision to turn her unmatchable drive toward helping those in need. We on the LOVESWEPT staff—Nita Taublib, Publishing Associate; Beth de Guzman, Editor; Susann Brailey, Consulting Editor; Elizabeth Barrett, Consulting Editor; and Tom Kleh, Assistant to the Publisher of Loveswept—vow to continue to bring you the best stories of consistently high quality that make each one a "keeper" in the best LOVESWEPT tradition.

Happy reading!

With every good wish,

Nita Taublib

Nita Taublib
Publishing Associate
LOVESWEPT/FANFARE
Bantam Books
New York, NY 10103

"Ms. Pickart has an unfailing ability to lighten
the darkest day with her special blend of
humor and romance."   --*Romantic Times*

THE BONNIE BLUE

by Joan Elliott Pickart

**Slade Ironbow was big, dark, and dangerous, a
man any woman would want — and the one
rancher Becca Colten found impossible to
resist!**

Nobody could tame the rugged half-Apache
with the devil's eyes, but when honor and a
secret promise brought him to the Bonnie Blue
ranch as her new foreman, Becca couldn't send
him away. She needed his help to keep from
losing her ranch to the man she suspected had
murdered her father, but stubborn pride made
her fight the mysterious loner whose body left
her breathless and whose touch made her burn
with needs she'd never understood.

AN 291 - 7/91

<u>FANFARE</u>

Enter the marvelous new world of **Fanfare!**
From sweeping historicals set around the globe to
contemporary novels set in glamorous spots,
Fanfare means great reading.
Be sure to look for new **Fanfare** titles each month!

Coming Soon:
TEXAS! CHASE
By *New York Times* bestselling author, **Sandra Brown**
The reckless rodeo rider who'd lost everything he loved...
Bittersweet, sensual, riveting, TEXAS! CHASE will touch every heart.

THE MATCHMAKER
By **Kay Hooper**, author of STAR-CROSSED LOVERS
*Sheer magic in a romance of forbidden love between rich and mysterious
Cyrus Fortune and the exquisite beauty he is bound to rescue.*

RAINBOW
By **Patricia Potter**
*A flirt without consequence . . . a rogue without morals . . . From a fierce,
stormy passion rose a love as magnificent as a rainbow.*

FOLLOW THE SUN
By **Deborah Smith**, author of THE BELOVED WOMAN
*Three women bound by the blood of their noble Cherokee ancestors . . .
one glorious legacy of adventure, intrigue -- and passion!*

THE SYMBOL OF GREAT WOMEN'S FICTION FROM BANTAM
Ask for these books at your local bookstore.

AN 293 - 7/91